I0557667

Byron Grush

Time Travelers Abroad

A novella

Copyright © 2020 Byron Grush
All rights reserved.

This book is a work of fiction. All characters, names, places, and businesses are the result of the author's imagination or are used fictitiously. An effort has been made to portray historical events, stories and myths of the time period as accurately as possible; however, any resemblance to actual events or persons, living or dead, is purely coincidental. No part of this book may be reproduced or transmitted through any means, electronic or mechanical, or stored in a retrieval system.

Cover background picture is 30 Doradus, Tarantula Nebula (captured by the Hubble Space Telescope), a public domain photograph.

Published in the United States by Broadhorn Publishing, Delavan, WI
ISBN: 978-0-9985454-5-5

Author's Preface

The subject is time. Time immemorial, time which will tell, time best forgotten. Time like a wheel, time as a paradox, time which is illusion and truth simultaneously. The time of our father's father's father's father's, etc. Father Time. Mother Time. The time of our life, the end times, the time of irreversible succession. Time that will come, time only imagined. Time according to Aristotle, Newton, Einstein, Salvador Dalí. The last syllable of recorded time. The time that flies and never does return.

Or does it?

More properly, it is space-time. Consider the earth as it orbits the sun at 30 km per second. Consider that the sun is hurtling through space at somewhere between 30 and 250 kms per second. The orbit of the earth as it is dragged along with the sun is a spiral, a huge corkscrew shape. Then think about the earth rotating around its own axis once every 24 hours. Now imagine a man in a time machine, setting the device to jump even a few seconds forward or backward in time. How does he end up at the same location where he started? That three-dimensional point is now many kilometers across the universe—a universe which itself may be moving. This phenomenon may be akin to the law of momentum. Momentum: the next time you are in a moving train, jump up. You will land on the same spot even though the train has moved. Space-time momentum? Space and time are inexorably linked, at least if you want to travel in a time machine.

Which brings us to the Many-Worlds Interpretation of quantum mechanics. As explained in Wikipedia (should you wish to look it up), the Many-Worlds Interpretation implies that there are many universes, perhaps an infinite number (is the term "infinite number" an oxymoron?). MWI demonstrates time as a many-branched tree, wherein every possible quantum outcome is realized. This is intended to resolve some paradoxes of quantum theory. It suggests that all possible outcomes of quantum measurements are physically realized in some "world" or universe.

Okay, so when the man in the time machine jumps a few seconds into the past or the future, does he end up in some parallel universe? Is that universe also in motion? Are the two systems of space-time connected absolutely or relatively? Or is there simply chaos? Does a jump into space-time cause any changes? Here we must leave science for science fiction.

Most science fiction (and here I generalize—which one should *never* do) depends on the suspension of impossibility, or should we say, the inclusion of some improbable element such as artificial gravity, bipedal human-like aliens, universal language translators, faster than light spaceships, or time travel. There is often an implied prediction that certain of these unlikely items will someday come to be true. In fact, some have: the first men on the moon for example. Reality, however, can take the fun out of the fantasy. We can no longer imagine moon people living on the dark side of the moon. Or can we?

This book might be thought of as a sequel. Last year I finally finished and published a novel of time travel which I called *The Death of Time*. It is a work of *historical* science fiction. That is, the main characters pop in and out of space-time where real people did real things. They meet and interact with historical figures and maybe try to change history a little. Or not. They discover parallel universes and versions of the future that could happen. Or not.

I originally started this short novel as a long short story called "After the Death of Time" in which I wanted to show what happened to some of the characters from the last book that I left figuratively dangling over a cliff. Somehow it got away from me and started writing itself into a longer work. I've enjoyed following along with the automatic writing. I just wish the muse could spell better. At any rate, here I present for your possible entertainment, several long short stories which are related and involve some familiar characters lost in time and space. Time travelers abroad in a universe of improbability.

Prologue

The man found the cat wandering through the yard. It looked lost and hungry, so he coaxed it with a bit of leftover breakfast bacon and brought it into the house. It was a large, long-haired gray cat with a notched right ear. But not feral, the man decided. The cat had devoured a tin of tuna fish, lapped up a saucer of milk, and then curled up on the man's couch for a nap, just as if she had been going through a similar routine in another house for at least one of her nine lives.

"What's your name, little lady?" the man asked the cat.

"My human called me Scheherazade, but that's not my real name," said the cat (in cat language which, of course, the man did not understand).

"I wonder what Roberta will say about you when she gets home."

"I can charm her. I don't worry," said the cat in a series of staccato meows.

The man, whose name was Jeffery Benson, switched on the television and settled down in his favorite chair, a well-worn overstuffed armchair that Roberta hated, which made him love it all the more. It had history. Some of that history was stuck down in the creases below the cushion—candy wrappers, an expired bus pass, some very stale popcorn, an old pair of reading glasses—history. The game he wanted to watch wasn't on yet. He could wait, watch the news for a while. Nothing much to do on one's day off in this town.

This town was Oak Ridge, Tennessee. It had originated around 1943 as a top-secret military area where research and development into the production of the rare isotope uranium-235 was its only industry. In a few years the town had over 75,000 residents, schools, theaters, restaurants, supermarkets, a library, churches, a sporting facility, and a symphony orchestra. Uranium-235 was essential for creating the world's first atomic bomb. Oak Ridge was producing material for the atomic bombs that would devastate Hiroshima and Nagasaki.

Two years after World War II ended, Oak Ridge became Oak Ridge National Laboratory under the civilian direction of the Atomic Energy Commission. No longer was it the singular commitment of the lab to produce fissionable nuclear material. Basic research into atomic energy caused repurposing of now obsolete equipment and a downsizing of nonessential personnel. Some of the remaining scientists were lucky enough to have research projects in their own areas of interest, with little or no interference by the powers-that-were. One of those scientists had been a man named Dr. Madison James McGinley. A fire had consumed his laboratory some time ago and now McGinley had disappeared. Dr, Madison McGinley had—well, you could not say owned—had lived with the cat named Scheherazade.

Jeffery Benson, who now intended to live with the cat (if Roberta didn't throw it back out in the street) was unaware of Scheherazade's origin and did not know Dr. McGinley. Jeffery did work at the Oak Ridge National Laboratory, but not as a scientist. He was part of the maintenance staff and arguably more essential than some of the scientists. He was a supervisor at building 24, not very near McGinley's old lab. He remembered the fire, but his own staff had not taken part in the cleanup. Thus there was no connection between Benson and McGinley except for Scheherazade.

He flipped through all four channels. CBS had the Bert Parks Show, NBC had the Ralph Edwards Show, and DuMont was broadcasting professional wrestling. ABC, where the Red Sox and Yankees would later be playing live, had a news program showing film clips from last night's Miss Universe pageant in Long Beach, California. The bathing suit competition was being shown when Roberta arrived home. Jeffery met her at the kitchen door.

"How was your bridge club meeting?" Jeffery asked.

"Oh, the usual," replied Roberta. "Anne Simmons' husband has sciatica, Dotty Logan is going to Florida next week with her cousin…the Mister is staying home, and Sandy Dresdner wants us to contribute to her church's missionary fund…I said not this year."

"Well, come into the living room. I have something to show you."

Scheherazade cracked open one sleepy eye as the couple entered the room (which was now *her* bedroom). Roberta stood looking at the cat for a time and then shook her head. "Mangy isn't it?" she said.

"Now Bertie, she was looking starved and lonely. I had to bring her in and feed her. We can take her to the shelter if you don't like her, but I thought…"

"You thought it would be nice to have a pet cat. I bet she has fleas! She's skinny and she needs a bath. What do you want to name her? Betsy Saunders has a cat named 'Fluffy,' but this one…maybe 'Scruffy' would be more appropriate."

"So we can keep her?"

"Put an ad in the Shopper-advertiser next week. She may belong to somebody. Meanwhile, we should clean her up."

Scruffy! Scheherazade thought about that one. Not a flattering name I don't doubt, she thought. Humans are so insensitive. We cats are magical animals. We go back to the Egyptians…further back! The Druids worshipped us and also the ancient Greeks. My ancestors could have cured Europe of the Black Death if they'd sent us to go after the rats. We were the familiars of witches. Fleas! The idea. I don't have fleas but that woman probably does. Oh well, a bath might be nice. Scheherazade looked up at Roberta Benson and meowed a hello-how-are-you at her.

"If we don't find the owner, I'll get her a nice new collar...pink with sequins," Roberta continued.

"Oh pul-eeze!" meowed Scheherazade.

Saturday of the following weekend the Bensons staged a cookout and invited a few of the neighbors. Jeffery was the proud owner of a brand-new grill called "George's Barbeque Kettle." It was a round, kettle-shaped charcoal grill with a dome-shaped cover that was being sold by a Chicago man named George Stephen who had invented it. Some people called it the Sputnik after the Soviet's space satellite. No one had thought of covering a grill before, but the results were quite good: the burgers juicy and the steaks done to perfection.

Jeffery had a selection of hamburger patties and all-beef franks ready to go as he waited for the charcoal to turn white on the surface. Roberta had prepared a big bowl of her (she claimed) famous potato salad and Denise, from next door, had brought baked beans. Bernie and Sarah Haas from down the block had brought a watermelon along with their two children, Janine and Ben, who had requested the melon. Later they would have a contest seeing who could spit the seeds the farthest.

Margery and Harold Jacob brought their dog, a dachshund named Wolfgang to the picnic. Scheherazade was not pleased. She hissed at the dog and Roberta snatched her up and put her in the house. This, for the cat, added insult to injury in the worst way. She could take that dog with one paw behind her back. For a while she looked out the window at the festivities. No table scraps for her. She began to look around and found an open window in the bedroom. The screen was not tightly fastened and a few quick pushes popped it open. Scheherazade was on the road again.

She kept to the bushes that lined the houses in the subdivision. Occasionally a dog would bark at her approach, but people kept their pets in the house or on a chain. Scheherazade was thinking as she walked about the days so long ago when she had lived with the alchemist. That had been several centuries back and life was not as interesting in the stuffy old castle then as it was here in the town of Oak Ridge. For one thing, the food was much better here and for another, the sofa was softer than her former perch on the alchemist's workbench or on his pile of old books. But she had liked the old man and she even had liked his dog, a large Irish Wolfhound.

It had been a nice sunny day so far, but the sky was now beginning to become overcast. Scheherazade hoped it would not rain before she found shelter. She could smell it in the air. She chuckled a cat chuckle (which sounds a little like coughing up a fur ball) as she thought about the picnic and those ignorant humans who would get rained upon before the watermelon was eaten and the seeds spit. She hurried down the street toward where she knew there was a service station with a row of garbage cans behind it.

The air around her was thickening into a gray mist. Scheherazade knew instinctively that something was wrong about it. She felt she was drifting within a thick brume in which nothing was visible. Her sense of up and down failed and she thought she was falling. No way to land on her feet when orientation was impossible. The nebulosity was complete. She was swept as if by a tidal wave of vapor into a new place. And a new time. For Scheherazade, the cat with one thousand and one lives, was being caught in a space-time vortex, a temporal anomaly, a portal between this world, and the many possible other worlds that exist simultaneously and adjacent to one another. Universes and times that overlapped accidentally—or maybe on purpose. And maybe she would travel back in time to see the alchemist again. Or maybe not.

AFTER THE DEATH OF TIME

It was a sweet little ball of blues and greens, covered in places with a fluff that swirled as a jealous moon pulled and pushed against the planet's slow rotation. Not so very different from Earth. Earth from long ago and far away, that is. Through the transparent wall of the time ship, Lorcan Mac Conmara watched the ball grow larger as they approached.

"It's about time we found a planet," Mac Conmara's young companion, Riordan Éamon Ó Ciardha, blurted out. "I'm really hungry."

"You should be," said Mac Conmara. "Your last meal was some fourteen billion years ago."

"I would say more like twenty-eight billion years," interjected Nikolai Borisov, the third man in the ship and its inventor and pilot. "We journeyed to the beginning of the universe, passed through the singularity into this alternate universe, and have been traveling at least an equal distance in space-time. And we could have just turned around and gone back home if you hadn't smashed the console."

Borisov addressed his indignation toward Mac Conmara, who had indeed attempted to stop the time machine from reaching the singularity known as the Big Bang. He had thought that if they engaged the singularity, their ship being in effect a speck of errant time-stuff that shouldn't exist at that crucial moment, they would cause the death of time and the universe would never form. He had picked up a loose piece of metal and swung it against the control panel. He had not stopped the machine from colliding with the singularity, however. He had merely disabled some of the controls.

Mac Conmara believed that Nikolai Borisov needed to be stopped. Borisov was a scientist from an era many hundreds of years into the future from Mac Conmara's own time. In a way, Mac Conmara was also a scientist. He had lived most of his life in Ireland in the sixteenth century and had studied the occult arts, especially alchemy. His companion, Riordan Ó Ciardha, had been his apprentice. Mac Conmara had been attempting, through alchemical means, to journey into other dimensions as he believed, from his reading of Hermes Trismegistus's ancient works, the Asclepius and the Corpus Hermeticum, that alternate universes existed and could be visited. Ironically, Mac Conmara and Ó Ciardha had been pulled into the mid-twentieth century through the malfunction of a time machine built by a scientist from that era named Dr. Madison James McGinley. The ensuing exploration of time which they experienced with McGinley's help, led them to the discovery of the far future scientist Nikolai Borisov's plan to time travel back to the beginning of time. How they had ended up where they were now is another story*.

Once they had determined that their course had them pointed toward a possible Earth-like planet, Borisov shut down the space-time drive and its semi-coupled faster-than-light drive. This allowed the spherical ship to float along gravity waves toward their goal. Beneath the floor they could feel the vibrations of the large gyroscope that kept the ship from tumbling.

When Riordan questioned the scientist as to why he had done this, Borisov answered by comparing his technique to a certain winter sport, which to him was ancient, but to the alchemist's apprentice was futuristic: curling. In curling the object was to give just the right amount of push to a large stone puck so it would slide along the ice and stop within a circular target.

"The idea is to let the natural momentum of the ship carry us just close enough to the planet to enter into an orbit around it. If I guessed correctly, we won't crash into it or go sailing right by," he explained.

"We will circle the planet? Like a moon?"

"Exactly. Then, before our orbit can decay…and that would be disastrous…we will do a small space-time jump and land on the planet in a good spot. Hopefully not in the sea or on a mountain top."

"But the controls…"

"That, my fine young friend, is where you come in. You will help me jury-rig the console so that we can achieve a degree of control. I believe I can bypass the damage your master has done to it."

---

* See *The End of Time* by Byron Grush, Broadhorn Publishing

"And me?" asked Mac Conmara. "What can I do to help?"

"You can make some sightings of the planet. We don't know what is down there yet. The ship has sensors which are still operative. Get busy while the lad and I sort out the mechanical problems."

The alchemist sat in front of a viewing screen and manipulated it using a joystick which allowed him a wide range of vision. His knowledge of astronomy came into play and he took notice of a curious thing: the constellations he could see just beyond the planet were a mirror image of those he had known on Earth. Then he focused on the planet's surface. There, through the clouds, he saw vast oceans and great land masses. And again, the continents appeared as familiar shapes but reversed. It was as if this new universe existed on the other side of a looking glass and they three were a triple manifestation of Alice Liddel, about to follow the white rabbit down a mysterious rabbit hole.

The alchemist, of course, had no knowledge of Lewis Carroll's famous book. He was from an age nearly three-hundred years before its publication. The mystique of tumbling into an unknown realm was so vivid and tantalizing that he seemed to be living in a parallel fantasy, recognizable at a deeply unconscious level. Now he increased the magnification of the view screen and suddenly let out a gasp.

"Cities!" he yelled to the others. "I see cities. Tall buildings like we saw in the twentieth century in America. Vehicles. And people! They look, from what I can tell, as if they may be human! Not bug-eyed monsters or sentient vegetables as you might expect." Then Mac Conmara described the reversed forms he had observed.

"It makes a kind of bizarre sense," said Borisov. "This universe may be the exact inverse of the one we left. If so, the planet is indeed Earth-like. We will be able to breathe the air and drink the water."

"When I was a child," said Riordan, "we thought the people in China walked upside down since they were on the opposite side of the Earth."

"It won't be quite that extreme," answered the scientist. "But we may be in for some challenges. Now, let's get to work on that console."

A day later, counting by Earth hours, three hungry, thirsty time travelers emerged from the time machine onto a verdant plain in a valley surrounded by snow-capped mountains. A carpet of brilliant purple and orange wildflowers extended in a pathway toward low foothills in what, judging by the position of the morning sun, was an easterly direction, but which, in a reversed world, was probably westerly. There had been few supplies in the time machine. They would need water and food. So far there was no indication of animal life that could be trapped nor of free-flowing water they could drink. The flowered pathway suggested the possibility of a river or a lake at its terminus, and so they followed it.

The foothills disappointed, no water source being found there. They ascended the low hills to continue their search but ran into a wall of rock at the base of the mountain which was too steep to negotiate. The alchemist and the scientist discussed returning to the time machine. They could look back at the valley where the machine sat, a black ball refusing to reflect sunlight; its walls were transparent from the inside, but opaque from the outside.

Meanwhile, Riordan wandered along the wall, partly feeling his way because the angle of the sun did not penetrate the gloom cast as deep shade by the towering wall of rock. He was about to abandon this effort when his hands encountered an opening. He nearly fell into what was apparently a fissure in the rock: a huge crack that must have originated many millions of years before. To his amazement, Riordan saw a shaft of light far into the crack—light at the end of the tunnel? He called to the others.

Certainly, they thought, the fissure would not extend the full length of the mountain's great mass, but it was worth exploring. The floor of the fissure angled upward toward the light, suggesting it was a passageway to…somewhere.

As they moved through the narrow, tunnel-like fissure, they got glimpses of the sky far above them at intervals where the crack was more vertical. Light illuminated their passage at these places, revealing that the floor upon which they climbed was set with paving stones. The fissure had been used by humans at some time in recent history—they hoped. There were chisel marks on the walls suggesting that the passageway had been widened.

The tunnel steepened and they found the floor had been roughly hewn into steps. These were uneven but a welcome aid for the travelers. At last they emerged from the fissure onto a long mesa that stretched out from the mountainside like a giant finger. Near the end of the mesa was a stone dwelling. They hurried toward this, hoping to find it inhabited.

Riordan reached it first. It was a box-like structure, nearly square, and constructed from the same hand-hewn stone that had been used to pave the tunnel. It had a flat roof, a solitary window that was not rectangular but had five unequal sides, and a doorway on which a wooden door swung slowly open and closed in the wind. Riordan peered inside.

In the darkness of the stone house Riordan could barely make out the shapes of what must have been furniture: a three-legged table and a round stool. As his eyes adjusted to the gloom, he saw that hanging from a ceiling rafter were several chunks of dark reddish-brown material. Drying meat? He did not see any sign of life. However, just to make sure, he called, "Hello? Is anyone here?" No answer.

When Mac Conmara and Borisov arrived at the house, Riordan was nibbling on one of the slabs of dried meat he had taken down from the ceiling rafter.

"How do you know that is safe to eat?" quizzed Borisov.

"I dunno, but it tastes sort of like chicken," Riordan said. "What do you think this place is? Nobody seems to be living here."

"Looks like a hunter's cabin or a retreat," answered the scientist. He watched hungrily as Riordan continued devouring his chunk of meat.

"Couldn't we just go back to the time machine and return to our own universe?" Mac Conmara asked the scientist.

"Well, there's a slight problem with that idea," said Borisov. "While it is true that we regained a modicum of control through our repair efforts, we are lacking in certain materials I would need to make a full-fledged restoration of the device. I would not trust it until we get some heavy copper wiring."

"That would mean going to one of the cities that we observed. But we landed in such an isolated area…"

"For reasons of security. We don't want the machine to be discovered by the natives. We'll just have to hike down off this mesa and try to find the nearest city. Hand me one of those pieces of jerky, would you?"

They climbed down the side of the mesa toward a valley where they could see the silver ribbon of a stream flashing in the sun. Loose stones made their way difficult, but they soon learned to address the slope at a slight angle, lessening the steepness of the descent. Back and forth they zigged and zagged until at last they stood on level ground. At the stream they scooped up handfuls of clear water to quench their thirst. They gave no thought to possible contamination—it was drink or dehydrate and possibly die of thirst! This parallel world did not seem to them to be hostile, even though it was a bit short of paradise.

They rested on the bank of the stream. Somewhere in the distance there was a grinding noise as if pieces of rusty metal rubbed together angrily. As it grew loader, they could discern the sputtering sound of a motor. Something was approaching. Riordan climbed a short way up the mesa to get a better look. When he returned he said:

"It's some kind of a vehicle. Similar to those automobiles we saw in twentieth-century America. But slightly different. Rather ungainly and rattling as it moves along what appears to be a road. It's coming this way. Should we hide?"

"I think not," answered Borisov. "We have to make contact at some point."

And so they awaited the arrival of the vehicle. True to Riordan's observation, it looked like a twentieth-century car or truck, but there were odd angles to its design. It appeared to be powered by a steam engine and belched clouds of smoke into the air. It was the color of rust and parts of it shook and rattled and threatened to fall off. It came to a stop just next to them. A door opened with a loud squeal and a man stepped out. He stood looking at them for a few minutes. Then he spoke:

"Dia duit!"

The time travelers just looked at each other. Riordan looked at the man more closely. To his amazement, he noticed that he had six fingers on each hand!

The man repeated his statement and added, "An dtuigeann sibh?"

"Oh my God," exclaimed Mac Conmara. "I do believe he is speaking Ghaeilge…Irish! I don't know how that is possible, but…let me try…"

And to the man he said, "Dia duit. Conas tá tú? Cá hainm atá ort?"

Borisov asked Riordan, "What's going on? What's he saying?"

"The man greeted us and asked if we understood him. My master said, 'Hello. How are you? What is your name.' It is Irish, but with an accent that is hard to understand."

"Is Éireannach mé," said Mac Conmara, "I'm Irish," indicating his country of origin. The man looked confused.

"Cé hiadsan?" The man asked, wanting to know who they all were.

The conversation continued with Riordan translating as best he could for Borisov. The man's name was Eoghan Nollaig. He lived down the valley in a small village and often came up to the mesa where he maintained a small cabin—the one they just visited—for hunting. He was about to retrieve some dried meat he had left there. Mac Conmara apologized and explained they had eaten some of it but would be happy to pay for it. He offered the man some of the coins he had in his pocket but upon seeing the money, which happened to be of twentieth century United States issue, the man again looked confused.

Mac Conmara tried to explain that they were travelers from a far land—without revealing just how far away it was. Would Nollaig be willing to take them to his village, he asked?

"Tá. Is breá liom é sin," he agreed.

They helped him carry the remining dried meat down from the mesa and the four climbed into the car. With a clang the thing bumped itself down the road toward Nollaig's village. The landscape they passed through was mostly barren with a few scrubby trees whose trunks had been twisted by the wind, and a number of large boulders that had rolled down from the mountain partly obstructing their way. Nollaig steered around the boulders with little effort.

"Ár detach," Nollaig said (our house) when they had pulled up in front of a two-story dwelling on a street lined with similar structures.

The houses were of a style that resembled the half-timbered structures of Earth's Tudor era: the dark wood framing was exposed in elegant crisscrossing and the spaces between timbers were filled with white plaster. The two travelers from sixteenth century Ireland felt an unusual familiarity upon seeing the row of houses. Familiar but unsettling. Something seemed a little off about this village and these human abodes. Viewed from a certain angle, the houses merged into a repetitious pattern that induced vertigo, even when the viewer had two feet firmly on the ground. Riordan was particularly affected and closed his eyes as he was led through the front door of Nollaig's "teach."

A dark-haired woman greeted them. Nollaig introduced her as his wife, Aideen. Riordan could not help but notice that she too had six fingers on each hand. She wore a long flowing dress that dragged on the floor as she crossed the room. Would they stay for dinner, Nollaig wanted to know? Certainly they had much to talk about.

The meal consisted of a stew of meat and vegetables which Riordan thought might be mutton, potatoes and turnips. A dark red wine was served in copper mugs and freshly baked bread completed the fare. The conversation revolved around where the visitors were from, where they were going, what the local village was like, what Nollaig and Aideen did for a living, if there were children, and if there was a big city nearby. Riordan translated for Borisov.

"We two speak Ghaeilge but our companion has only English and Russian, so we must translate," Mac Conmara told Nolliag,

"I do not know of these languages. I understand you well, however," Nolliag responded. "You asked how we toil. Well, I am a maker of casks and boxes of wood, while Aideen teaches at the school for orphans. We have no children of our own, so it is rewarding that she can do this work. And you?"

"Nikolai and I study science. He invents things and I am a scholar of sorts. Riordan is my helper…apprentice. Riordan and I are from County Cork, which is very much like this village. What did you say it is called?"

"Glanbaile. How far away is this County Cork? I have never heard of it."

"Oh, it is very far. We came here in a vehicle which is now over on the other side of the mountain. It broke down. That is why we are asking about larger towns that may have the things we need to repair it."

"You could journey up along the river to Dubhuisce. It is twenty miltes distance for walking, but perhaps you might hire a boat. You must stay with us tonight and embark early tomorrow."

Lorcan Mac Conmara rose earlier than the others. There was a lot on his mind. He walked up the street to ponder the situation and to see some of the town before they left. Cobblestones were laid with tight accuracy on the avenue and sidewalks of larger stone squares separated the houses from the street. Curiously, there were houses only on one side of this main street; the opposite side was a tangle of green vines with sharply pointed leaves and ugly thorns. Encountering a man coming up the street toward him, Mac Conmara inquired of him why the townspeople did not remove the vegetation. The man just stared at him.

When Mac Conmara approached the jungle of vines for a better look, the man grabbed him by the shoulder. "They sting. Did you not know that?" the man told him. "Very dangerous."

Mac Conmara thanked him and shook his hand. He walked further up the street to find a row of shops. One was a bookstore with tomes in the window whose bright covers identified them as histories. Too bad his American money would not be recognized here. He would have loved to have acquired some of these books. When he returned to the house he found Nolliag setting the breakfast table.

"Poor Aideen," Nolliag said, "is not feeling well. She has come down with a virus, I am afraid. We will have to fend for ourselves this morning."

"Nolliag," Mac Conmara asked, "is there any way to exchange my foreign money for currency I can use here?"

"I tell you what, I will trade you some money for your coins, as they are of great interest to me as tokens of our meeting. They will remind me of your stories of County Cork. Anyway, you will need money to rent a boat and a captain to run it."

"You are most kind. We will remember you, and perhaps return once we obtain the supplies we need. I don't know how I can ever repay your kindness."

"It is all in the nature of good fellowship to help one's acquaintances. Good deeds will return to those who do them to others"

Mac Conmara could not possibly know the irony of this statement, but soon, all too soon, he would begin to realize that something was very wrong on this planet.

More of a barge than a boat, it had a large paddle wheel at the rear and a steam engine which occupied most of the main deck and which, with a furious noise akin to that of a wounded elephant, threw acrid clouds of gray smoke into the air. She was named Ceo Diahal, which translated as "Fog Devil." Nolliag had accompanied the time travelers to a dock up the river from the town. Green mold grew on pilings that looked like decaying teeth. They hailed the boat's captain who stepped cautiously from boat to dock, then came to see what they wanted.

"Captain Olmo," said Nolliag, "I've brought you some customers who'd like a pleasure trip up to Dubhuisce, that is if you be willin' to take them."

Captain Gavin Olmo smiled broadly, displaying a set of teeth that matched the green pilings in an ominous manner. “Yer in luck,” he answered. “I’m about to cast off for that very destination. Have they any experience on a boat?”

“Well,” said Riordan, “we might be good at navigation.” Mac Conmara gave him warning look which said, don’t reveal much about us. Riordan took the hint. “But no, we’re not exactly sailors,” he added.

“Well, hop aboard and be lively now. Have you no luggage? By the by, the fare will be…”

Nolliag complained when he heard the amount Capain Olmo wanted to charge and he began to haggle. After all, it was his money they were spending. Finally, the price agreed upon, the time travelers boarded the Ceo Diahal and Nolliag waved goodbye.

“He’s looking a bit peeked,” commented Riordan. “I hope he’s not caught what his wife has.”

“And I could say the same for us,” said Mac Conmara.

Borisov just sneered. “I wouldn’t worry about it,” he said. Mac Conmara wondered about that.

Landlubbers or not, Captain Olmo put the time travelers to work, casting off, coiling up ropes, hanging over the bow to watch for snags. There was only one crew member, a lean youth named Niall who hardly looked old enough for the kind of work required to run the boat. Nonetheless he stoked the boiler with firewood while the skipper stood at the wheel and eased the Ceo Diahal into midstream. The big paddle turned, churning the water and scattering fish in all directions.

The deck was filled with crates of odd-shaped fruits or vegetables—Riordan wasn’t sure which. Their glossy purple skins reflected the morning sunlight. The boat picked up speed. It passed along a shore from which jutted makeshift piers where small boats were docked. Other craft began to appear on the river: light skiffs with sails of deep crimson or chrome yellow and intricate designs: abstractions of birds or fish. Captains hailed each other

Soon the semirural scenery gave way to thick forests. Water birds stood on long legs near the shore dipping beaks into the water to spear golden fish. Other birds flitted among the tree branches, their brilliantly colored feathers reflecting sunlight like sparkling stars in a galaxy of greenery. Riordan, fascinated, struggled to identify the avian flock but failed. Also of interest to the apprentice was a school of silvery blue fish that followed the boat, fins like decorative lady's fans breaking the surface. Nature strangely familiar, yet so foreign.

The stoker, Niall, temporarily idle, came to sit on the rail next to Riordan where the apprentice was acting as lookout. A conversation commenced involving the origins and experiences common to adventuring young men. Suddenly, Niall grasped his stomach and bent over in pain. Riordan reached for him but the youth collapsed onto the deck, rolled onto his back and began to convulse. Riordan yelled for help.

Lorcan Mac Conmara and Captain Olmo rushed to the bow but the ship's hand was dead, white foam crusting around his mouth, a look of agony in his eyes.

"Go mbeannaí Dia thú," said Captain Olmo, giving him God's blessing as he closed the lad's eyes.

"What happened?" asked Riordan. "Why did he die?"

"Aye, 'tis some strange malady, for certain," answered the Captain.

Mac Conmara gave a questioning glance to Borisov who had just come from the other side of the boat. The scientist shrugged. "Better cover him up," Borisov said.

It was late in the day when they approached the docks at Dubhuisce. Birds that might have been gulls circled the wharfs, their chatter drowning out the sounds of the busy riverfront. The Ceo Diahal was heading directly for an empty pier. Too fast, thought Mac Conmara. He glanced back at the wheelhouse but did not see Captain Olmo standing there. Gasping, he ran to investigate and found the Captain lying on the floor, white foam pouring from his mouth.

Mac Conmara jerked the lever that controlled the coupling of the engine to the paddlewheel, but it was too late. The Ceo Diahal crashed into the pier, splinters of wood flying, cargo catapulting into the river. The time travelers were jostled and thrown to the floor. The boat tilted and began to sink. Riordan and Borisov jumped onto what was left of the damaged pier. Mac Conmara followed just in time as the Ceo Diahal sank heavily, pushing out around it a wake that rocked nearby ships.

A crowd gathered. Soon a man in uniform questioned them; perhaps he was a guard or a policeman, the travelers thought. Their explanation that the Captain and his deckhand had died suddenly from some strange illness was not received as credible. The uniformed man commanded them to follow and ushered them to a van-like vehicle. A drive through narrow streets brought them to the center of the city where tall buildings were set back from the roadway by small, tree-lined parks.

They were brought before a man seated at a high desk and again they were questioned. An investigation into the cause of the accident would be made, they were told, and they would be held in custody until such time as a determination could be made as to their possible culpability. They were taken to jail cell and left to wonder about their fate.

The cell was not spacious, it was windowless, and enclosed on three sides by what looked like concrete blocks. On the front was an expanse of iron bars and a barred door. The bars were rusty and old. At least they could see out in the direction of a hallway patrolled by guards. They attempted to engage the guards in conversation, but this proved difficult as the guards kept their distance. Hours passed with no word from the authorities.

A guard came with three plates of food on a tray. Bread with something that might have been ground meat made into a salad spread. This was passed to them through an opening in the barred door too small for anything larger than a plate. Mac Conmara asked the guard for news. The man lingered for a few moments, talking casually with his prisoners but could shed no light on the proceedings that affected them. It might be days, he admitted, before the investigation would even begin. His name was Keegan Caolán and he lived at the far end of town where less expensive lodgings could be had. He was anxious to return home to his wife and three children once his shift was over, but he would come back before he left with what he could find out. They did not see him again that day.

They did not see Caolán the next day either. In fact, they saw no one until late that next evening. No food or water had been delivered to them. No one appeared in the corridor although they yelled and banged on the bars with the empty plates from yesterday's meal. Finally, a light came on and a figure walked down the corridor toward them. It was not Caolán.

"Where is Caolán?" asked Mac Conmara.

"Dead," said the man. "He's died of some strange illness that came on suddenly. Poor chap. Everyone is getting it! The magistrate went to his bed this afternoon as well. He gave instructions to release you if you agreed to reenter custody in one week's time. We haven't the staff to maintain your imprisonment, so…"

The new guard unlocked the door to the cell. "God speed," he said and then began to cough violently. "Ah, damn, now I've got it! Go quickly now."

Riordan, Mac Conmara, and Borisov lost no time exiting the police station. Out on the sidewalk people moved about at a normal pace for that time of night. Couples strolled arm in arm. Men and women came from restaurants to hail taxis. It seemed like a normal evening for a big city. And yet the number of illnesses, some fatal, that they had encountered was troubling.

"Is it an epidemic, do you think?" asked Riordan.

It may be," said Mac Conmara. "We lived through the times of the Black Death…you might have been too young to remember, Riordan. It came on suddenly like this, although people lingered for days before expiring. Covered with black and purple buboes they were. Most of it was on the continent, but Ireland saw many deaths as well. Horrible and terrifying. It originated in the fourteenth century, but it kept coming back. Some say half of Europe was wiped out."

"Fleas," said Riordan. "It was transmitted by fleas that rode on the backs of rats that traveled in sailing ships. I read history as well as science when I lived for a time in the twentieth century. There was a horrible epidemic in that century, too. They called it the Spanish Flu. In 1918 it killed more people than the Great War had. In Chicago it started at a Naval base…again it came over the seas. Do you think this planet is experiencing a pandemic?"

"I would not worry so much about that," said Borasov. "There had been a great many pandemics on your old Earth. After the one in the twenty-first century that killed so many people, science began to tackle the problem with a renewed effort and an expertise that virtually eliminated such illnesses. By my time, we had genetically improved the human race with an immune system that that was no longer susceptible to viruses."

"That is all well and good for you," countered Mac Conmara, "but Riordan and I are not from your time. We could catch this thing."

"I don't think so. Don't forget, we are not only not from this planet, we are from another universe. I don't think it can affect us."

"Just the same, I think we should get busy repairing your ship and getting the hell off this planet!"

"That we will. Let us find a store that sells electronic goods. Let us walk, the night is still young."

The darkness was pierced by strategically placed streetlamps, glowing globes atop tall poles that flickered from flames of wicked oil. They were able to get a better look now at the buildings of the city. The tallest were only about twenty stories, dwarves to the great skyscrapers of Earth. Their design was stringently symmetrical with walls of polished stone and rows of those curious five-sided windows. The roofs were peaked or adorned with spires that gave the city an Earth-like medieval feeling. The ground level was given over to store fronts, restaurants, theaters, or parking garages. Mac Conmara held Riordan back several paces from the scientist. They needed to talk.

"Do you get the same feeling I do…about the Professor?" asked Riordan.

"You mean that he is holding something back. Something he knows but is not telling us."

"That's right. He is so certain that we will not contract the illness. Why?"

"I have a theory, and I do not like saying this, but perhaps we are not only immune…"

"But we are carriers of the virus! We are the fleas that have brought plague to this poor planet! We have killed them all!"

"Not necessarily. We don't understand what the illness is. It is killing people, true. But maybe only some. It is essential, however, that we get off this planet as soon as we can. Keep a sharp eye on Borisov. I still don't trust that man."

They found no stores selling electronic supplies, nor televisions nor radios, nor electrical appliances. It was becoming obvious that the technological evolution of this planet was not on a par with Earth although it was so similar. There were no airplanes and the automobiles they had seen were powered, like the boats, by steam. Finally, in a shabby quarter of the city, they came upon a store that could have been described as a country store or as an early version of a hardware store. Through the dusty window they could see coils of wire.

"It's not insulated," commented Borisov, "and it may not be of the proper conductivity, but it will have to do."

"What do we do? Wait until morning when the store opens?" asked Riordan.

"I think not," said the scientist, picking up a rock and smashing the window. He grabbed a coil of wire and said, "Run!"

No one was chasing them, but they hurried around the corner and ducked into a small park set back from the street. There were few trees in this park, and they had come to hide in an open space. This seemed unwise to Mac Conmara. The alchemist watched Borisov with suspicion as the scientist took a small rectangular object from his pocket and held it out in front of him.

"What on Earth is that?" Mac Conmara asked.

"A remote," said Borisov as he pushed a button on the device.

There was a whirring sound and the smell of ozone assailed their senses. Suddenly in front of them, a large, dark, spherical shape materialized. The time machine had come!

"What…you could have done that at any time?"

"Yes, and I can do this also," said Borisov as he jumped through the open door of the machine and slammed it shut. The alchemist and his apprentice looked on in disbelief as the time machine disappeared, leaving them stranded on a planet where a plague was rapidly spreading.

"That bastard!" said Mac Conmara.

* * *

The caravan had iron-bound wooden wheels painted bright red and green in spiral designs with silver stars around the rims. Its large, arched roof was shingled in red wood and a tin chimney poked out of it in which a bird had tried but failed to build its nest. There were five-sided windows on the painted yellow sides and a round door at the back with steps that folded up during transit. Two donkeys—or four-legged animals that resembled donkeys—pulled the caravan along a dirt road through a forest that skirted the foothills of a nearby mountain range. Crows—or large black birds that resembled crows—circled above the caravan, perhaps acting as guides or sentinels for the humans.

On the driver's seat sat a man dressed in rough leather garments and a battered straw hat. Inside rode his wife and two daughters who tried but failed to entertain two men, an alchemist and his apprentice. Mac Conmara and Riordan, down in the dumps about their abandonment by the scientist, Borisov, had hitched a ride with the Gypsies—or a family of nomads who resembled Gypsies—after many long days of traipsing through the forest south of the small town of Glanbaile.

After being marooned by the scientist, the time travelers had wandered through the streets of the larger city of Dubhuisce, keeping their distance from people they met in order not to infect them (if it were truly the case that they were carriers of the disease.) They resorted to stealing food and water and hid from the authorities. As they lived this way for the next few weeks they were dismayed to find that death also wandered through Dubhuisce. A brutal Danse Macabre was diminishing the population at an alarming rate.

They journeyed to Glanbaile to see if Eoghan Nollaig and his wife, Aideen were still alive. Sadly, they learned that the couple who had been so kind to them now were buried in a mass grave at the edge of the town. About a quarter of the townspeople had survived the epidemic. Apparently, some were immune to the plague. These survivors treated the time travelers with distrust, not wishing to take the chance that they would not start the epidemic up again. Mac Conmara and Riordan decided to leave Glanbaile, perhaps to find another region of the country which the Danse Macabre had not visited.

The family of Gypsies was named Ó Brádaigh. Father and mother had given names of Colum and Muirgel respectively. The daughters were ten year-old Caitríona, who they called "Cat," and sixteen year-old Ríona, who seemed to have a crush on Riordan. Colum Ó Brádaigh had come upon the time travelers on the forest road, exhausted and hungry. He insisted they climb into the caravan. When they objected, stating the possibility of infection, Colum told them that he was sure that his family and he were immune, having traveled through several afflicted towns and localities without mishap.

"You may deem 'tis not in the cards that we be struck down by this horrible plague," he explained. "You look in need of succor, so climb up and let the Missus tend to your thirst and hunger."

As the caravan rumbled along the dirt road, Cat and Ríona performed a folk dance for the time travelers while the mother, Muirgel, strummed a lively melody on a mandolin. Ríona danced close to Riordan, drawing her silk veil across his face seductively.

"Come on, smile," she said to him. "It's not the end of the world."

I would not be so sure, Riordan thought to himself. It was difficult to overcome the deep depression that had befallen the time travelers. This perky young girl helped a little, but Riordan and his alchemist master shared a foreboding of ultimate disaster concerning the fate of the planet, and an unshakable guilt of being its genesis.

"Are there any doctors in these towns that can study the disease and come up with a cure?" Riordan asked.

"The doctors have no cures," answered Muirgel, "but they tell the people to avoid contact with each other. They say gathering in crowds is dangerous. But the people will have their fêtes. They mingle in the marketplace. They do not believe the doctors."

"What do the leaders say?"

"The leaders encourage the people to keep working together, generating wealth for the landowners, paying taxes which support the politicians. I am afraid for our people if they listen to the leaders instead of the doctors."

A poem that Riordan once read during his stay in the twentieth century on Earth came to mind. It was by Vachel Lindsay and it was called, "The Leaden-eyed."

LET not young souls be smothered out before
They do quaint deeds and fully flaunt their pride.
It is the world's one crime its babes grow dull,
Its poor are ox-like, limp and leaden-eyed.
Not that they starve, but starve so dreamlessly,
Not that they sow, but that they seldom reap,
Not that they serve, but have no gods to serve,
Not that they die, but that they die like sheep.

Mac Conmara went to sit next to Colum Ó Brádaigh on the driver's seat. They were emerging from the forest and approaching a small hamlet. On the outskirts of the town were signs of devastation: wagons piled with ominous sheet-wrapped bundles lined the road. A deep pit could be seen not far from the wagons. Wisps of black smoke rose from the pit. A laborer with his face covered by a piece of dirty cloth came toward them.

"Go back," the man cried. "There's nothing for you here."

Colum shook the reins and urged the donkeys to a trot. Passing through the town quickly was a good plan, immunity or no immunity. In the village proper they observed the ruins of buildings that had been torched, smoke still rising from blackened timbers. Suddenly, a gang of men started following the caravan. They carried axes and pitchforks which they swung wildly. Colum brought the donkeys to a run. Soon they were clear of the town.

"We have to pass this way," said Colum. "I want to get to the seashore and it is the only route. There will be others of my race there and we may be safe…if all goes well."

They came to another town, this one the size of Dubhuisce—and a once thriving metropolis. The streets were empty of people save for a lone figure that Mac Conmara recognized as a counterpart of his own century's Plague Doctors. The man stood silently but with a morbid swaying like dead reeds brushed by light wind—wind mixed with the miasma of decay and corruption. He wore a wide-brimmed black hat, a black robe, and a black facemask that resembled the beak of a carrion bird, a crow or a raven. The design was not, Mac Conmara knew, to symbolize a harbinger of death, but to allow for a hollow area in which to place herbs thought to ward off the poisonous microbes in the air. Still, it was a frightening vision

He turned toward them as they passed, then slowly turned away again and slunk toward a deserted building. The empty city was an eerie reminder of the potency of the virus. It shocked the senses and ushered a new wave of despair upon the hapless alchemist. He could do nothing for the dead and the dying…nothing except escape a similar fate if that were possible. He thought again about the scientist, Barisov. The man had known that one or all of them had carried the disease from an alternate universe to infect this sad planet. If he could meet up with him once more…

Back inside the caravan Riordan asked Muirgel why she and her husband were so sure he and Mac Conmara would not infect them or their people. By way of answer, Muirgel held up her hand: it had five fingers.

"You are one of us, one of our race. Not like the Others. We do not get the sickness of the Others," she explained.

"I hope that is true. But I worry."

Riordan considered revealing their actual origins to Muirgel. But telling her they were from another dimension—an alternate universe—

was problematic. He would not be believed and it would only put a strain on their relationship with these new friends, friends they needed for survival. If the gypsy race really was immune to the pandemic they had brought, they could be comfortable living within their society. If not…

* * *

Riordan and Ríona had spread a blanket out on the grassy bluff overlooking the beach next to the Gypsy village. Ríona was now eighteen and she no longer annoyed Riordan with her girlish advances. Indeed, it was Riordan who now pursued Ríona. In the two years that the time travelers had lived with the Gypsies, Riordan had watched the young girl blossom into a lovely, sensitive young woman. He found he cared for her and wanted to spend as much time with her as he could. Ríona's crush on Riordan had evolved into full-fledged adoration. She was certain that he was her soulmate, that they would spend the rest of their lives together. Riordan wasn't quite to that stage yet, but he was falling in that direction.

Out in the bay the fishing boats jostled for the best location to cast their nets. Gulls—or some white birds that resembled gulls—circled above expectantly. Ríona lay with her head on Riordan's lap and gazed up at the passing clouds, perhaps seeing an animal or a bird portrayed in the billowy vapors.

"Tomorrow is the fête," she said. "The people will come from all around to celebrate the harvest season. There will be dancing and music and games, and the children will play on the beach building sandcastles. When it gets dark they will shoot exploding things into the sky with many colors and loud sounds."

"Fireworks. It is strange," said Riordan, "that you invented gunpowder but have no guns or cannons. Like the early Chinese, I guess."

"Chinese?"

"What about the Others? Do they use weapons of any kind?"

"No," she answered. "They usually are so peaceful. Although lately…. It is sad what happened to the Others. Their world will never be the same."

"I've heard," said Riordan, "that there are roving bands of plague survivors that raid the villages of your people."

"Our people. You are one of us too."

"Our people. But I worry about conflict. If we could welcome those survivors into our midst…"

"They have regressed into savagery from the shock and strain of the plague years. They are still in denial about their own behavior, how that led to the deaths of so many. They blame us for our immunity. They will never be welcome until they change…which they may never do."

"That is sad. We are so happy here. If there was some way…"

"You have too big a heart! Save it for me, my love."

On the beach, an animal that might have been a pig turned slowly on a spit over an open fire. Delicious aromas mixed with breezes of fresh sea air to entice the fête-goers. A caldron of water bubbled and sputtered as buckets of shellfish were dumped into it. Ears of a corn-like plant sizzled on a grill made from discarded metal. It would be a feast to be remembered—and not just for the food.

Lorcan Mac Conmara stood watching the dancing. The women wore colorful full skirts which they lifted as they swirled to the rhythmic music. The men tapped with hard leather shoes tipped in metal against a wooden floor that had been laid over the sand. The musicians played stringed instruments that resembled banjos or beat upon drums with mallets. Suddenly, a man pulled Mac Conmara away from the dancing.

Mac Conmara listened to the man whose name was Calbhach Beirne. Beirne was frantic with news of a hunt from which he had just returned. He had spoken to Mac Conmara before anyone else because he had sensed in the time traveler a worldliness and a wisdom which none of the other of his people processed. Mac Conmara would know what to do.

"In the high hills beyond the village," Beirne said, catching his breath, "we were after wild muc when we came upon a strange thing. It was practically hidden by the stinging vines which had grown up around it. I've never seen a thing like it!"

"Take it slowly, man," said Mac Conmara. "What was this thing?"

"I do not know. It was larger than a man by three times, completely spherical, and black with a blackness that seemed to defy sunlight. We were frightened and ran back without finishing the hunt."

"Tell no one else just yet. We do not want to spoil the festivities. But I want you to take me to see this thing before it gets dark. Will you do that?"

Before Beirne could answer, a cry came up near the fringes of the celebration. Suddenly, stones the size of a man's fist fell from the sky. Someone yelled, "A raid! The Others come!"

Riordan and Ríona had been examining the pile of fireworks that were to be set off that evening when they heard the cries. A band of Others was rushing across the beach toward the fête. They were dressed in rags and had painted their faces with red lines. They carried clubs and slings which they used to hurl stones at the fête-goers. Their yells sent shivers up Riordan's spine. The fête-goers were weaponless and, taken by surprise as they had been, would certainly fall before the onslaught.

"Run!" said Ríona.

"No, wait," said Riordan. "Quickly, bring me a lighted torch from the cooking fires while I set up some of these rockets."

Ríona ran to fetch a torch. Riordan had seen that the fireworks consisted of crude rockets that would shoot up into the sky when lit. He reasoned that they could be aimed at the oncoming hoard of Others. He positioned several and as soon as Ríona returned, he lit the fuses. The Others were nearly upon them as the first of the rockets fell, exploding and spreading flaming gunpowder among them.

"Okay, said Riordan, "now we can run!"

The fête-goers scattered in all directions as the Others, although singed and burned by the rockets, nonetheless persisted in the attack. There was chaos everywhere. Mac Conmara saw Riordan and Ríona across the beach and beckoned to them. They ran to the alchemist's side. "We must fight," said Riordan. "No," said the alchemist. Mac Conmara urged them to come with him. Calbhach Beirne, he told them, would lead them to the site of what he believed was the time machine.

"It appears," he told them, "that Barisov never got off the planet. It may mean we have a chance to get it operative…however…"

"If the Professor couldn't make it work, how will we be able to start it up. And where is he?"

Mac Conmara, Riordan and Ríona trudged along behind Calbhach Beirne as Beirne led them through mounds of sand and of dense grass toward the foothills. Up they climbed, looking back at the beach where the battle was still underway. Ríona's people, many having fled, were now the minority and the tide was turning toward conquest by the Others. Their prize would be a kettle of cooked shellfish and it would be won at extreme cost.

It was late afternoon by the time they reached the time machine. It was nearly totally encased in the loathsome stinging vines. A few yards away, on the edge of the vine jungle, they found Barisov. He lay motionless, his body wrapped in the vines and pierced by sharp thorns.

"He must have come out of the ship for some reason and fell into the vines," Riordan said. "I wonder why?"

"I think when he left us stranded he hadn't repaired the ship enough to leave the planet. He simply moved it some miles away from the city in order to do the repairs and then to leave without us. He landed in the vines and came outside to try to remove them…and you see the result. He didn't know their sting was lethal."

"So how are we going to get into the time machine?"

All this time Beirne had stood dumbfounded. The talk of leaving the planet in a ship—a time machine no less—had left him confused and incredulous. When he saw that the alchemist and his apprentice were getting closer and closer to the stinging vines, he turned and ran. Ríona too was confused, but she waited, and called out the Riordan to avoid the vines.

"I think we can pull Barisov free without getting stung," said Mac Conmara.

"But why would we want to do that?" asked Riordan.

"He has something I think will help us. Find me a fallen tree limb and bring it here. We'll lever him out."

A few minutes later the scientist was free of the vines and lying in a heap while Mac Conmara went through his pockets. "Ah," he said, "here it is." He held up the small rectangular device the scientist had called a remote. "Now if we can figure out how to work this…"

While the alchemist examined the time machine remote, Riordan took Ríona aside and attempted to tell her the truth about themselves. He could tell by the look on her face that she did not believe him. But then, as Mac Conmara let out a loud "Ah ha," she witnessed the large, round, black thing that they had called a time machine—vanish! A second "Ah, yes" from the alchemist accompanied the unbelievable materialization of the machine a few yards away from them, and Ríona fainted.

Once she revived, Riordan showed her inside the time machine. She saw how the walls were transparent from the inside but opaque from the outside. She saw the complicated looking control panel. She watched as Riordan activated the viewing screen and focused it on the beach where the attack had now subsided. There were bodies everywhere. Most were her own people. Her parents and sister were not among them—at least she could not see them among the dead and injured.

"You'll be going back to your village now, Riordan told Ríona. "I'll go with you to see you safely there, but I must come back here and help my Master get this machine running."

"I want to stay with you. You are going to fly away in that thing, aren't you?"

"I think so, if it still works. But you have a life here…a family and friends. I will miss you, but…"

"I'm coming with you, and that's that! It's not wise to argue with your mate so early in the relationship, don't you know that?"

Ríona was on the verge of tears and Riordan was torn. He wanted to be with her enough to consider staying on the planet. And yet, he wanted to return to Earth as well. Meanwhile, Mac Conmara suggested that they bury the scientist. The alchemist understood the conflict in his young apprentice. He doubted he could leave a new-found love if he were in the same situation. But how to advise the youth? Best busy themselves with the tasks at hand, he thought.

"It looks like Barisov patched the panel with this new wire before he died," said Mac Conmara when they reentered the time machine. "I watched him at the controls when we were journeying to the Big Bang and I think I can operate this thing. Of course, it might explode or send us hurtling into the nearest star…"

"We could just stay here," said Riordan.

"I'm going to start the countdown. You have about ten minutes."

Riordan looked deeply into Ríona's eyes. She returned his look of love and anguish. Then he knew what they must do. "We are going with you," he said. Ten minutes later the time machine vanished from the surface of the planet with three passengers.

The Voices of Time

It is a pleasant early June day in 1952 in Oakridge, Tennessee. Mockingbirds play tag in the sky above Bear Creek Valley. There is little traffic on the streets of the small town, only a few small children on bicycles or Radio Flyer scooters; school is out for the summer and camp is still weeks away. A solitary man sits on the front porch of a comfortable bungalow on Chariot Lane rocking in an antique rocking chair he had purchased at an estate sale enough years ago that he now fits it like Yogi Berra's hand fits his well-worn catcher's glove (the man is a Yankees fan). His favorite team will be playing against the Saint Louis Browns later today, and the man is planning to listen to it on his radio. The starters for the Yankees, besides Berra, will include Mickey Mantle in center field, Phil Rizzuto at short stop, and Allie Reynolds as pitcher. But for now, he rocks and watches his cat stalking a young cottontail in the front yard.

The cat is named Scheherazade, after the fabled storyteller in one of the man's favorite books, *The Arabian Nights Entertainments* (the translation by Sir Richard Francis Burton). Most cats have nine lives, the man knew, but this one had one thousand and one. She had come to him in a most unusual way: by traveling through space-time from her home in Ireland where she had lived in the laboratory of a certain 16th century alchemist named Lorcan Mac Conmara. Very few people are aware of this strange fact. If it were known, and believed, she would be as famous as Schrodinger's cat.

The man, now nodding off in the warm breeze, is Dr. Madison James McGinley, once upon a time a scientist for the Manhattan Project and lately an independent research specialist into quantum theory. He has his own area here at Oak Ridge National Laboratory where he had created a machine which seemed to be able to retrieve objects from past eras. The machine has been destroyed in a fire and McGinley's funding has been eliminated for the project.

Just as well, he will tell you. Some things are better left alone. Time travel can be perilous and the chances of changing time potentially disastrous. The wings of a butterfly, it is said, may cause a hurricane on the other side of the world. And McGinley can, but will not tell you just how close our world had come, once upon another time, to the death of time itself.

The rabbit sits nervously twitching its nose. It thinks standing still will render it invisible to the cat. Scheherazade creeps slowly toward it, knowing that a sudden movement will panic the rabbit, send it scurrying away, too fast to catch. Cause and effect. In another moment, just like Schrodinger's cat in its debatable box, the rabbit will be either dead or alive. Or both. Then, ruining the experiment, someone comes up the front walk and hails McGinley, and the rabbit hops away.

McGinley opens one eye; he has a visitor. She is Natsumi Ito, from down the street. Mrs. Ito is a widow with grown children who have moved away, and she is lonely. She has known the good professor for six years and often comes to call on him, bringing cookies or a nice warm slice of pie. McGinley likes cherry, sometimes strawberry rhubarb. Natsumi prefers pecan with a caramelized top. Today she brings no offering. Today she has a strange story to relate. Madison will know what to make of it, she hopes.

Natsumi Ito, her husband, Akihiko, and their children, Ayane and Miku had come in the late 1930s to the settlement in the Bear Creek Valley that would eventually become the town of Oak Ridge and the site of a secret wartime research laboratory. Akihiko had found work in construction. The town was about to mushroom into a thriving community, but the Itos would not profit from its development. In 1941, Japan bombed Pearl Harbor. In 1942, the Ito family, like many Japanese Americans, were hustled off to an internment camp.

Camp Forest near Tullahoma, Tennessee, was primarily a training facility for the infantry, artillery, and other military divisions. In 1942 it became a prisoner of war camp housing Italian and German POWs and about 200 American civilians of Japanese ancestry, all without access to legal process. The Itos were sent to Camp Forest to await possible relocation, but somehow they were lost within the system and would remain there until the end of the war.

Tar paper covered barracks, sometimes without shower or toilet facilities, overcrowding, questions about ancestry, demands to sign loyalty oaths, loss of personal and real property, the insult of watching German prisoners come and go for labor release while they remained behind barbed wire, these indignities were heaped upon 110,000 to 120,000 Japanese Americans in camps all around the country, of whom about 30,000 were children. When finally released, detainees were given $25 and a train ticket to their former place of residency where their homes and business no longer existed. The Itos returned to Oak Ridge. The Radiation laboratory was still growing. Akihiko found work once more as a laborer. One day, an earth moving machine overturned and killed him.

"Hello, Natsumi," McGinley says once both eyes have opened and blinked away the fatigue and reverie that had held off wakeful awareness.

"Madison," the woman says in an anxious voice like the rattling of pine needles in a high wind, "you must come!"

"What seems to be the matter?"

"You see. Come now." She starts back down the walk and up the street. McGinley nearly falls on his face struggling to hurry from his rocking chair. He follows.

She leads him through the front room toward the back of the house. McGinley can't help feeling the contrast between this woman's pin-neat environment and his own disorderly domicile. Nothing modern, no Scandinavian design end tables or futuristic pole lamps. Only sensible furnishings from another era which still served and were well kept. No stacks of old magazines as one might see at McGinley's residence. No clumps of cat fur waiting for the dustpan. Just a vacuumed braided rug over a waxed hardwood floor in front of a sofa dressed in ruffled slip cover, a coffee table that wasn't quite Art Deco, a few incidental pieces, and two colored prints of watercolors on the wall, one of a Japanese village on a mountain side, and another of an arched wooden bridge over a small brook.

In the kitchen a freshly baked blueberry pie sits cooling on a metal table. The sink holds the yet unwashed implements of cookery. Uncharacteristic of her not to have cleaned up, but something had interrupted her diligence. She leads Dr. McGinley to the kitchen door and she stops, points, then backs away. "There," she says. "What is that?"

That is a phenomenon that McGinley recognizes and from which he recoils, saying only, "Oh no, not that!" For the gray-white swirling mass of mist at the other side of the kitchen is a time vortex. A rupture between the normal universe (at least what passes as "normal") and the myriad possible alternate instances of space-time. It is a doorway of a sort through which one might travel through time and space. It is indeterminant and dangerous. And its existence is all McGinley's fault.

In the spring of 1953 (in an alternate reality) and simultaneously in 2153 (because time intersects at certain space-time instances), two teams of scientists activated devices to generate a rift in time. Enrico Fermi and Leona Libby worked at Argonne Laboratory in 1953 while McGinley, stranded in the Empire States Building in 2153, had just completed his own time fragmenting device. Switches were thrown at the precise moment when the two space-time instances coincided, and our Earth's very first space-time whirlwind appeared as the result. McGinley (of this current reality), had thought the phenomenon no longer existed. Now he sees that he was wrong.

It is a space-time rift," McGinley tells Natsumi. "Stay well back. It should dissipate shortly."

But of course, it does not dissipate shortly. In fact, two slender tentacles of time-stuff emerge from the whirlwind, snake across the kitchen, and wrap themselves around Natsumi and McGinley. In an instant, they are pulled into the whirlwind. Round and round they go and where (and when) they will stop…

In the agricultural landscape of Germany's Thuringian Basin lies the town of Gotha, founded in medieval times. On a low hill in the city center is situated the Friedenstein Castle, which dates to the mid-seventeenth century and is the original residence of the House of Saxe-Coburg. The first and largest Baroque palace built on German soil, its Protestant design is simple, purposely contrasting with typical Catholic palaces of the period. It has four wings of unequal size and height, four towers, and the only extravagance of decoration is the placement at each of the four corners of the monumental statues of Moses, Elijah, John the Baptist and Martin Luther.

On the north side of the castle is the Orangerie. There are two houses for the plants here on either side of a well-tended park made in the style of an English garden. A man walks here every morning, brooding upon his own storied history. He lives here in exile at

Friedenstein Castle, under the patronage of the Duke of Saxe-Gotha-Altenburg. He spends much of his time here writing.

He once was an important figure in the Bavarian town of Ingolstadt where he was born and served as a professor of civil and cannon law. There in 1776 he founded a secret society based in part upon the philosophy of the Enlightenment and the ideals of independence of thought and judgement as expressed by Immanuel Kant. Then he was known as Brother Spartacus.

His name is Johann Adam Weishaupt. His Society was the Order of Illuminati. Although he recruited many members, some through his membership in a Masonic lodge, his philosophy was met with great resistance by the establishment. He preached "illumination, enlightening the understanding by the sun of reason, which will dispel the clouds of superstition and of prejudice," but, unlike the Kantian practice of freedom of thought, his Society prescribed strict adherence to the belief system of its superiors. His writings were deemed seditious, and the Society was banned by the government. Weishaupt soon lost his position at the University of Ingolstadt and fled Bavaria.

It is May of 1815. Weishaupt is about to return from the Orangerie to the castle proper when a strange gay mist begins to form in front of him. Out of the mist step two figures, dressed in unusual costumes. A man and a woman. They seem startled and disoriented. Weishaupt approaches them and asks them, "Was tun Sie hier? Wer bist du?"

"He is speaking German," McGinley tells Natsumi. "We are somewhere in Europe in a past era. Don't be alarmed, he appears friendly." McGinley looks around for the mist but it had disappeared. No exit. Then to Weishaupt he asks, "Sprichist du Englisch?"

"Yes, I do. I'll repeat…what are you doing here and who are you? You are English?"

"American. My name is Dr. Madison McGinley and this is Natsumi Ito. We are…ah…travelers from the state of Tennessee. I am a scientist and Mrs. Ito is retired. We are interested in this wonderful castle. Is it yours?"

"The Friedrichstraße is the property of Emil Leopold August, Duke of Saxe-Gotha-Altenburg, a great patron of the arts. I live here by virtue his kindness. It was his father, Ernest the Second, who was known as Quintus Severus in the Society, who first granted me asylum. You see, I am Adam Weishaupt…you have heard of me? No? I am working now on my *Complete History of the Persecutions of the Illuminati in*

Bavaria. I founded the Illuminati in the same year that your country gained its independence. A remarkable coincidence, don't you think?"

"That is quite interesting. I should be pleased to hear more about you and your society. And to see the castle. Do you think that would be possible?"

"Perhaps. The Duke entertains many visitors. Carl Maria von Weber, Johann Wolfgang von Goethe, Caroline Louise Seidler, to name a few. He is the author of *Ein Jahr in Arkadien: Kyllenion*, a poetic novel. There are two young British women here now, stepsisters, I believe. A Claire Clairmont and a Mary Wollstonecraft. The latter has many friends in literary circles…Percy Bysshe Shelley and George Gordon Lord Byron, I understand. They are on their way to Lake Geneva, Switzerland, early next year, although I hear the weather will be terrible!"

As they walk to the castle lagging a bit behind Weishaupt, Natsumi says to McGinley, "But Madison, I don't know if we should…"

"The only way we can get home," McGinley tells her, "is to wait for the whirlwind to reappear. We need an excuse to stay around here for a while. This is the 19th century, somewhere in Germany. Don't worry, it's just a matter of time. So to speak."

Near the main gate an arcade runs along that side of the four wings of the palace. One or two relief carvings can be seen on the façade, looking as if they had been salvaged from some older building. Above the entrance is a curious, but familiar emblem: a circle surrounded by rays of light, inside of which is an equilateral triangle containing a single wide-open eye. Natsumi bumps McGinley's arm.

"Madison, it's like on the dollar bill," she says.

"The Eye of Providence,' says Weishaupt. "I did not know American money had this design on it. When did that occur?"

"Uh, it's from the Great Seal of the United States. Our founding fathers designed it and eventually it was put on our money," answers McGinley. He isn't aware, however, that the dollar bill did not show the Great Seal until 1934.

In the main hall or Hauptsaal, they wait while their presence is announced to the Duke. The butler or diener had gazed askance at the time travelers' attire before flitting off to find the Duke. On the walls are hung large gilt-framed portraits of men in the costumes of long-gone time periods. McGinley guesses these are former dukes and the ancestors of the present one. Curiously, there are no paintings of women. There is one empty spot, indicated by a clean area on the dusty wall.

"What is missing there?" McGinley asks Weishaupt.

"It was a hunting scene. Very bloody with dogs ripping apart a fox. The Duke took it down long ago. He detests hunting."

Natsumi says, "It is as if we are in a dream."

"Perhaps it is best to believe that. Do not be surprised by anything you see or hear. Just go with the dream theory," McGinley says.

Finally, the butler returns and they are ushered along the hallway to a room probably intended as a day parlor or sitting room, but it is larger than McGinley's entire house. Inside they see two young women, apparently teenagers, dressed smartly in traveling clothes. They are seated together on a divan. Standing just next to them is a large figure dressed in a luxurious flowing gown, a bell-shaped skirt with embroidered floral bouquets, deep scooped neck line and a double string of pearls. Natsumi gasps because…

"It is a man," she whispers to McGinley.

It is, they learn as Weishaupt begins the introductions, Emil Leopold August, Duke of Saxe-Gotha-Altenburg. He enjoys dressing in women's clothing, apparently. The young women are Claire Clairmont and Mary Wollstonecraft. McGinley's eyebrows rise. He struggles trying to remember where he heard the name, Wollstonecraft, before. Then he asks:

"Mary Wollstonecraft. Wasn't your mother a famous novelist?"

"She was. I never knew her, however. She died just after I was born. She wrote *The Vindication of the Rights of Woman*. Very timely, don't you think?"

"Mary!" scolds Claire Clairmont.

"Revolution is in the air, dear sister-in-law," returns Mary.

"And you are obsessed with your dead mother!" Claire now addresses McGinley and Natsumi: "She spent most of her girlhood roaming through St. Pancras churchyard where her real mother is buried. She doesn't like her new mother at all."

"Churchyards are so comforting," says Mary. "The dead never complain. And anyway, I walk there with Percy. We talk of literature and the arts."

"Percy! Your would-be lover is a married man."

"Junge Damen! Young ladies! Please!" says the Duke. And to his newly arrived visitors he says, "Don't you just love it when young girls have spats? It is so delicious!"

McGinley decides to change the subject. "You young ladies have been traveling through Europe?" he asks.

"We are on a six-week tour," responses Mary. "Through some of France, though the getting there was fraught with much discomfort."

"Yes," says Claire, "crossing the channel in a violent sea is no picnic. The sailors suggested that instead of Calais, we should head for Boulogne! We had high wind and thunder, but we made Calais at last."

"The French," says Mary, "do not have the manners of the English, although the lower orders do treat you unaffectedly as their equal. From Paris we journeyed to Provins in the Île-de-*France* region. They were much better behaved there."

"There was another small village…remember it, Mary? There they were unaware that Napoleon had been deposed. They had not rebuilt their little cottages for fear they would be attacked by Cossacks!"

"Well, we saw Bar-sur-Aube, Chaumont, Langres, Besançon, Maison Neuve, Pontalier, rode through lush green valleys and wide plains, but finally we quit France for Switerland."

"Oh yes," says Claire, "I much enjoyed sailing on Lake Geneva. We shall return there, will we not?"

"We shall. The Swiss cottages are much cleaner and neater than the French, and the inhabitants exhibit the same contrast. The Swiss women wear a great deal of white linen, and their whole dress is always perfectly clean. I believe this superior cleanliness is chiefly produced by the difference of religion."

"We went then by boat to Germany," says Claire, continuing the story. "The banks of the river were beautiful although the river itself was full of rocks the avoidance of which was difficult for the rowers. We stopped at Strasburgh and at Manheim."

"I thought the countryside was uninteresting," says Mary, "with the exception of the area around Manheim. Then at Mayence we switched to a bigger boat. It was shaped like a steam-boat, with a cabin and a high deck. Most of the other passengers chose to remain in the cabin. That was fortunate for us, since nothing could be more horribly disgusting than the lower order of smoking, drinking Germans who travelled with us. Students, I guessed. But we glided thrillingly down that part of the Rhine that Lord Byron so beautifully described in his third canto of *Child Harold*: '…I am as a weed, flung from the rock, on ocean's foam, to sail where'er the surge may sweep, the tempest's breath prevail.' The current was rapid and dangerous, and we saw along the shore many hills covered with vines and trees, craggy cliffs crowned by desolate towers, and wooded islands, where picturesque ruins peeped from behind the foliage, and cast the shadows of their forms on the troubled waters."

"Oh, Mary," says Claire, "you describe it so poetically. Worthy of Byron. Worthy of Shelley. You should write it all down and publish it."

"I have thought of writing my remembrances. Perhaps even my fantasies. Along those lines, I have a question for you, Adam Weishaupt. Tell me of your town, this Ingolstadt of Bavaria. There is a great castle there where once lived an alchemist, I have heard. The alchemist experimented with galvanism, did he not?"

"It is a beautiful old city on the banks of the Danube, enclosed by a medieval defensive wall. The old castle, the Herzogskasten, was completed in 1255. But I never heard of an alchemist living there."

"Certainly there are experiments on dead bodies taking place in the city," says Mary. Claire looks at her, aghast.

"At the University there is the Ingolstädter Alte Anatomie, the old anatomy building. They do dissect corpses there, it is true. The church does not take kindly to the practice. We of the Illuminati, however, believe that any pursuit for scientific purposes must be tolerated."

"What is this galvanism?" asks Claire.

"It is a demonstration of the electrical properties of the nervous system," answers Mary. "They have attacked electrodes to the legs of a dead frog and applied current, causing them to kick as if in life. It is quite suggestive, do you not think?"

"But we are ignoring our new guests," says the Duke. "Do tell us of your travels. Are they as exciting…and poetic…as those of the young ladies?"

Oh boy, here we go, thinks McGinley. How do you tell people you have traveled through time? And yet, how do you lie convincingly without being found out? He looks at Natsumi; she is turning pale.

"I tell you," he says, "my companion is feeling a bit ill. Our journey has been arduous, perhaps not unlike these ladies have described of their sea journey. I wonder if we might take a rain check…I mean, postpone our conversation for a while so we might get a little air. Walk in the gardens to revive ourselves."

"An excellent idea," exclaims Mary Wollstonecraft. "I shall accompany you. Claire?"

"I'll stay here with the Duke and Mr. Weishaupt. You go and enjoy yourself. Maybe there is a cemetery around here someplace."

"May I suggest," says the Duke, "that you view our Wasserkunst…our water feature on the northern slope. Also the Hertzpgin Lustgärtlein on the west side is very nice this time of year. Roses of many varieties are to be seen in the Lustgärtlein. Then come back and we will do as the English do: drink some tea. We Germans are as well-mannered as you British."

"I hope I have not offended you with my criticism of the disgusting German students on the boat," says Mary.

"Not at all. You are, however, a bit opinionated. No matter. But hurry, your new friends are already out the door."

McGinley and Natsumi are heading up the Hauptsaal as fast as they can without looking like they are escaping. Natsumi says, "That young woman…is she…?"

"That is the future Mary Shelley, the author of the horror story, *Frankenstein.* She will begin writing the novel when they return to Lake Geneva. It will be the year of the eruption of Mount Tambora which will cause a colder than normal winter and a dismal summer, and which will cause Mary and her poet friends to remain indoors and tell ghost stories. Please don't let on that you know this. We don't want to change history…particularly if it erases that great novel from the future!"

They are standing at the circular fountain, the Wasserkunst, watching water spurting out from the mouths of stone frogs and lizards when Mary joins them. The spray from the center of the fountain is caught by the wind and hurled at them in a fine mist. The mist thickens to a milky haze through which they can no longer see. McGinley groans. It is the whirlwind, the space-time vortex that is swallowing them up once again. This time it has also grabbed Mary Wollstonecraft.

Jacques de Moray has risen early, unable to sleep. He is now in his early 70s and his long gray beard is a tangle of matts in which, his squire jokes, a family of French field mice will soon be residing. He has donned his white surcoat, emblazoned with its rose-red cross pattée, and has thrown a white mantle over his shoulders, also having the distinctive cross that identifies him as a member of The Latin Rule (also known as The Poor Fellow-Soldiers of Christ and of the Temple of Solomon, or as the Order of Solomon's Temple, or as the Knights Templar. or just as the Templars). Moray is not just any Knight Templar, he is its current Grand Master, the 23rd of a long line.

Moray leaves the Great Hall of the Tour du Temple where he has been pacing up and down for an hour and descends the terrace rampart to the courtyard. The four-story tower building flanked on its corners by cone-roofed turrets looms above him like a storybook's medieval castle sans dragon. The Templars domain is located outside of the Paris city walls and is a small city in itself, containing a Gothic style church, a smaller chapel, a cloister, the Master's own house, dormitories, kitchens, stables, farm land, a hospital, and a buttressed, ten-meter high crenellated wall flanked with fifteen turrets.

There is much on his mind. Earlier he had returned from Cypress to Poitiers, France, where the new Pope, Clements V, being himself a Frenchman, has moved the Papacy. His Holiness has requested a meeting to discuss a merger between the Knights Templar and the Knights Hospitallers, who are to be represented by their own Grand Master, Fulk de Villaret. Neither Moray or Villaret is in favor of the merger. But as the best laid plans of mice…be they French or otherwise…go astray, Villaret has been delayed and the Pope has been stricken with gastro-enteritis. So Moray has traveled to Paris where yesterday he was at the Maubuisson Abbey to be a pall bearer for Catherine of Courtenay, the Latin Empress of Constantinople and sister-in-law of King Philip IV. Such duties for an old man!

So many jealousies, so many intrigues. King Philip IV of France has been deeply in debt to the Templars who control a vast financial empire, the latter having virtually invented banking. The King would welcome the merger of these two military orders of the Church, desiring to command them himself as Rex Bellator, or War King (and wipe out his debt). Philip is also at odds with the Papacy. His attempts to tax the clergy had been so opposed by an earlier Pope, Pope Boniface VIII, that the Pope had attempted to have Philip excommunicated. Philip had Boniface abducted, charged with heresy, and, although the Pope was rescued, His Holiness died soon after from shock. The next Pope, Benedict XI, was allegedly poisoned by Philip's councilor, Guillaume de Nogaret. Pope Clement V is not about to mess with King Philip IV.

Only last year when riots erupted in Paris over the devaluation of money, King Philip feared for his life and sought refuge in the Temple's compound. Jacques de Moray had welcomed him and given him shelter. But now there is a conspiracy afoot to condemn the Templars for impropriety and more serious matters. Moray has asked Clement to investigate the charges and clear the Templars. The Pope initially agrees that the rumors are baseless, but the King intervenes, seeing an opportunity to destroy the Order and seize their assets. He plans mass arrests and an inquisition and will pressure the Pope to cooperate.

A walk in a garden in early October, when only a few flowering plants remain, when the leaves have yet to explode in a frenzy of color, when the grass, although still verdant, seems darkly asleep, when swallows and avocets and martins flock for imminent migration, is a walk of remembrances, not anticipations. Moray thinks back on grander times, his reception into the Order, campaigns in the East battling Egyptian Mamluks, plans for a major new Crusade. To recapture Solomon's Temple, their first headquarters at the Temple Mount in the Al-Aqsa Mosque in Jerusalem—what glory there would be in that!

His gate is lethargic. His awareness is flaccid. He wavers between reverie and fantasy. So that when a thin wisp of shadowy substance forms in his path like an adumbration of atmosphere warning of things to come, he hardly takes notice. It broadens, becoming more substantial and swirling like a dust devil in the desert. Now he sees it. Now he thinks, "O Jerusalem, Jerusalem, thou that killest prophets…." Now he backs away as the whirlwind spits out its passengers. Naturally, he makes the sign of the cross.

Mary Wollstonecraft is the first to emerge. Seeing the Tour du Temple and its environs she thinks it is part of the Friedenstein Castle. But the strange figure before her, dressed like a knight from medieval times, this doesn't fit. It is as if the last piece of the jigsaw puzzle is from another box. She blurts out:

"Hey there, is there a costume ball I hadn't heard about?"

"Comment vous dites?" he asks, not understanding her English.

"Tu parles français, mais vous ne parlez pas anglaise," she says, assuming the man is French and does not speak English.

Now Natsumi Ito pops out of the mist, nearly falling on her face. "Oh!" she says. "A Crusader! What century are we in this time?"

Mary has still not been informed about time travel and the space-time vortex that has just transported them to another era. "Why, it is the nineteenth century, of course," she answers, querulously.

"I don't think so," says Natsumi.

By this time Dr. Madison McGinley has arrived and the mist has dissipated. Jacques de Moray is dumbfounded. "Ça ne tient pas debout," he says; it makes no sense.

"Miss Wollstonecraft," McGinley says, "I will explain. But first, would you be so kind as to translate for us? There are a few things we must learn, and I think time, so to speak, is of the essence."

After some back and forth they learn that this is the Knights Templar compound just outside of Paris, it is October 13, 1307, and that the picturesque figure standing here is Jacques de Moray, Grand Master of the Order. Mary introduces herself and her companions as English travelers lately from Germany, but as McGinley cautions her, she omits the date she believes it really is. The man is obviously deluded or lying about the date, she figures. How to explain the change of scene however…

"Être tiré par les cheveux est déplorable," she tells the Grand Master. It is a French expression that means something like you're pulling my leg and I don't like it."

Before he can answer, Natsumi says to Mary, "Ask him if this is a Friday…Friday the thirteenth." She does, it is, and Natsumi says, "I thought so. I've read about this time in history. This will be one unlucky day for Monsieur Moray!"

"Pourquoi est ce jour…unlucky?" asks Moray. It seems, although not fluent, he knows some English.

"Natsumi," cautions McGinley, "remember there are certain things…"

But Natsumi, rattled, rattles on, "The King, Sir Knight, is sending soldiers to arrest you and the other Templars. It will happen this morning. You will be imprisoned and accused of horrible crimes. You will deny these and they will torture you until you all relent." Mary translates this for the Templar.

"C'est ridicule!" says Moray. "The Pope a rejeté these accusations."

"The Pope will bend to the King's wishes in this. You will be accused of spitting on the Cross, of homosexual practices, of worshiping an idol consisting of a mummified severed head..."

"Of John the Baptist, yes I have heard these vile lies. But you...tu es un sorcière! You foretell mensonges, untruths."

"I haven't told you the worst of it yet. They will take you to a small island in the Seine and you will be burned alive at the stake. You must run from here...now!"

"This is absurd," says Mary Wollstonecraft. "Who put you all up to this ridiculous play acting? Was it Claire? Or that preposterous Duke August? Enough is enough!"

"I hate to tell you this," says Natsumi, "but this is all very real. Here they come!"

King Philip's special guard has converged upon the Templar compound and they can be seen up near the Tour du Temple, lances and swords at the ready. Some of the Templar Knights have already been bound with heavy rope and stand close together in a circle. McGinley now voices his opinion: "Run!" he says.

They race to the Church of the Holy Mary, the Templar's largest structure besides the tower. From the air, most medieval cathedrals resemble the Christian Cross, symbolic in architectural design. This church looks more like a drawn sword: a long nave running west to east like the blade of a broadsword, the transepts like a crossguard, the choir like a handle, and the ambulatory like a pommel. As they run along the nave they hear the clatter of the King's men coming behind them.

There is a semicircular aspe at the east end and there they can see a gray-white mist beginning to form. It is another space-time vortex and just in time to save them, or so McGinley hopes. "Quickly," he says to the others, "into the mist!" Mary and the Grand Master balk. Natsumi pulls Mary into the whirlwind with her. McGinley shoves Moray into it and follows. But the whirlwind is not ready to dissipate and move on. It thickens and rotates and takes its own time (so to speak) before spitting its passenger out into another era. Time enough for a squad of the King's special guard to enter the vortex in pursuit of the Templar Grand Master.

Captain of the Guard Jean-Michel Lesauvage picks himself up from the thick bed of giant ferns he has been deposited upon by the space-time whirlwind and looks around. Members of his squad are strewn about the landscape, slowly recovering from what had been a harsh dumping of the armored men. Some have lost their helmets; all are dazed and disoriented. This is not the Church of the Holy Mary, thinks Cyril Côté, one of the soldiers…somehow we have entered a forest! A forest in the outskirts of Paris the likes of which I have never seen before.

There are impossibly tall conifers arrayed along an escarpment at one end of the low, bowl-like dale in which the squad now begins to regroup. Yellow-leafed ginkgos surround them; large gray-winged things are roosting in these trees—moths the size of eagles! There is an eerie silence broken only by the rattling of armor as the men move through the fern dell to climb to the ridge.

"What enchantment is this?" asks Côté.

"The mist," suggests another soldier named Alexandre Abel, "was chimerical, created by the sorcery of the Templar!"

Jean-Michel Lesauvage takes a count of his men once they reach the ridge of the pines. Besides Côté and Abel, he finds his company also includes only three others: Joachim Duchamp, Rainier Lyon, and Hadrien Mathieu.

"Whether or not this is an illusion," Lesauvage tells his men, "we are here for a purpose…to capture Jacques de Moray. Duchamp, you and Abel head in that direction, Lyon and Mathieu go that way, and Côté and I will go this way. Give a hail if you see the fugitive and his companions. Meet back here in one hour."

They split up into three directions. Red tunics disappear into the dense forest. There is little sunlight in the woods to reflect from their armor or to flash against their drawn swords. There seems to be no animal life except the occasional insect: beetles with metallic shells, flying dragonfly-like insects that Lyon calls snakeflies, slithering many-legged centipedes—all of them over-sized, at least to the experience of the Frenchmen.

Lyon and Mathieu are ascending the gentle slope of the ridge toward the north (we shall call it north, although the exact direction cannot be known since no compass has been brought). The tall conifers are beginning to thin. The brush underfoot is less dense. Lyon trips over something. It is a low circular structure which has been constructed from dried branches and other vegetation. It is about three feet across. Within it they see:

"Eggs!" says Lyon. "It's a damn nest. And look at the size of them! Ostrich, do you think?"

"There aren't any ostriches in France, dummy," says Mathieu.

"Well, anyway, we aren't going to be hungry. Make a nice omelet."

"Wait, look…one of them is hatching!"

A minute crack has appeared along the surface of one of the eggs. Other cracks splinter off from this like a miniature spider's web. They widen. Something dark green is inside. It jerks against the shell and suddenly, a head appears. Not that of an ostrich, however.

"Well, I'll be damned! It's a damn lizard. Crocodile, do you think?" asks Lyon.

"There aren't any crocodiles in France, you idiot," says Mathieu.

"Well, there are now!"

Duchamp and Abel are descending the ridge toward the south (at least, in the opposite direction from Lyon and Mathieu). To the east, as the height of the pines is diminishing, a view of a vast plane becomes apparent. Now in the sky they can see dark shapes circling; perhaps it is a flock of large birds. The wings of these creatures, however, are broad and leathery. They have long beaks and short, featherless tails. The soldiers imagine these are large bats. Very large bats.

"I hate bats!" offers Abel.

"Agreed," says Duchamp.

One of the flying creatures sloops down and snatches something from the ground. It rises again with a small animal in its jaws. The struggling animal is fur-covered and resembles, to the soldiers, a badger or a beaver. But not quite a badger or a beaver. The other "bats" chase the one with the prize. They are gone from view.

"I don't understand exactly where we are," says Abel.

"Ours is not to question our duty," say Duchamp. "I must say, however, that I never saw France looking like…"

Off in the distance now a herd of animals is running across the plane, kicking up dust which somewhat obscures their shapes. Deer? No, much larger than deer. As they come near the soldiers can make out silhouettes of creatures the size of oxen, but with long necks and tails that drag on the ground and—could those be feathers? They have lizard-like heads. They can only be:

"Dragons!" shouts Duchamp.

Lesauvage and Côté have gone east (with respect to the directions of the others) and have climbed down a tatus slope just reaching the edge of the plane. They can see the dust in the distance raised by the herd of lizard-headed animals. These are too far away to be of concern. As they scan the horizon they think they see the forms of other human beings on a small hill not too far away. It may be those they seek. Lesauvage sends Côté back to summon the others of the squad. He will wait and observe.

On the not-too-distant hill four people are also waiting, watching the dust and the herd of animals approaching. McGinley is explaining the reality of their situation to Mary Wollstonecraft who is translating for Jacques de Moray.

"We may still be in France," he tells them, "or not. But certainly, this is neither the fourteenth nor the nineteenth century. My best guess is that we have been transported into the Mesozoic era, possibly the Triassic or Jurassic. Those are definitely dinosaurs out there. I'm no expert, but it looks to me as if they are fleeing from some predator. Something large and frightening. Allosaurus or Tyrannosaurus Rex, I would think. We don't want to be around when it shows up!"

"I know not these words," says Moray. "This enchantress (he points at Natsumi) is casting spells. She has the look of a Saracen. If only I had girdled my broadsword upon my person before leaving my quarters! Without it I am helpless. These dragons that approach…these I would slay. After dispensing the witch, of course."

"What did he say?" asks McGinley.

"He thinks Natsumi is a Muslim," answers Mary. "I'll try to calm him down."

"At the moment," says McGinley, "I think we had better make for that stand of trees over there. The predator dragon has just arrived."

A massive shape can now be seen trailing the stampeding herd and it is slightly gaining on them. It is, as McGinley has surmised, a Tyrannosaurus Rex. Many times larger than the prey it pursues, the terrible lizard lumbers along on its two powerful hind legs, barely in a hurry, for it knows instinctively that the weaker dinosaurs near the rear of the herd will soon faulter and become an easy meal. Needle-like teeth protrude from its drooling mouth. It's tiny forelegs dangle almost uselessly from its chest.

One of the fleeing dinosaurs falls and the T-Rex lunges. It is over in a matter of minutes. Gore drips from the dinosaur's jaws. McGinley and company have started their retreat to the forest which is, perhaps, one hundred yards distant. The T-Rex, satiated only partially, swings its large head in the direction of the humans. New game! Small game, but easy to catch. Hunger drives the dinosaur as this is its nature. It abandons the herd and heads for the humans.

Cyril Côté has returned to the top of the ridge where the company is to reassemble. No one is there. He calls for Lyon and Mathieu but gets no response. He hikes through the forest in the direction those men have taken, calling as he goes. When he comes to the place where the nest of eggs had distracted Lyon and Mathieu from their mission, he sees that the lower vegetation has been trampled by something heavy. There is a path of sorts leading away consisting of small shrubbery that has also been crushed and he follows this. He sees dark red splotches at intervals. Then he enters a small clearing, stops, vomits, and lets out a sound that is half scream, half sob.

The mangled bodies of his companions lie upon the ground in a pool of congealing blood. Legs and arms and other bits of them are strewn around as if something had torn them into pieces and flung the parts about in an angry rage. It is a frightful scene. Côté, realizing that there is nothing he can do for them, backs away. What could have done this? He turns. It, the thing that perpetrated this horror, is standing before him, blocking his escape route. He is frozen in fear and cannot move. The creature stares at him, anger burning in its eyes.

It is a stegosaurus, an armored dinosaur which is a vegetarian, but a fierce fighter when it comes to defending itself and its progeny. When it came upon the two soldiers bending over the nest where it had laid its eggs, the creature chased them down, battered them with its spiked tail, and ripped them apart with its sharp beak-like mouth. Along its back are leaf-shaped plates and more sharp spikes. It is low to the ground on short legs but still stands as tall as Côté. It begins to swing its tail as if it is a dog, wagging in happiness upon seeing its owner. Only it is not happy.

McGinley and the others have just about reached the forest. The Tyrannosaurus is several yards away but coming at them fast. Suddenly there is a roar and a crashing as the trunks of the trees just before them are splintered. Out of the forest comes another dinosaur. It charges at the T-Rex. If McGinley had his dinosaur manual with him, he could identify this one as an Allosaurus.

T-Rex is a terrible predator, but it is not the current King of Pangaea. Allosaurus is just as big and just as bad. Allosaurus is thirty feet long, stands twelve feet high, and weighs two and one-half tons. Our T-Rex is slightly smaller, not being full grown. Both species are ferocious fighters. Both species are territorial. There is about to be a battle which, at least for the moment, will save the lives of the humans. They do not stay to watch.

Jean-Michel Lesauvage has been observing all this from his vantage point in a tree not far from where the others have entered the forest. He is outnumbered, but nonetheless climbs down from his perch with sword drawn and confronts the time travelers.

"Jacques de Moray," he yells, "I arrest you in the name of King Philip, The Fair."

"If I had my broadsword," responds Moray, "I would relieve you of the fat head of yours. That little pig sticker you hold would do you little good."

"Captain," says Mary to Lesauvage, "we have more pressing problems at the moment. One of those…dragons…is going to win the fight. We need to retreat!"

The group heads deeper into the forest. Moray and Lesauvage continue bickering. As they trudge through the brush Natsumi walks close to McGinley.

"Madison," Natsumi says, "we may not escape or be able to return home. I want you to know…I have always thought…you and I have both been alone so long. I admire you and cherish your friendship. Maybe…maybe if we do get home…"

McGinley is not used to expressing his feelings. He has been what is called a confirmed bachelor partly for this reason. He admits in his own mind that he does indeed have feelings for Natsumi. Now would be a good time to tell her. As good a time as any. But he hesitates. He looks into her eyes and, for the woman, this says more to her than McGinley can bring himself to verbalize.

Lesauvage has led them back to the basin of ferns where he and his squad had materialized. They have put a great deal of forest between themselves and the battling behemoths, but there is little security in that open place. It is where, he argues, the rest of his company will return soon. At least there will be strength in numbers.

Mary translates this for Natsumi and McGinley. McGinley agrees. If only the whirlwind would return, he thinks to himself. That is our only possible salvation.

Joachim Duchamp and Alexandre Abel had watched the Tyrannosaurus chasing the herd of smaller "dragons" and had seen the four fugitives running to escape from it. They had watched the battle between the two dinosaurs with a mixed sense of awe and disbelief. But now they have snapped out of their dazed state. Time to go. They retrace their steps back to the ridge and then descend to the bowl where the others are waiting. Strength in numbers? Three men with rapiers—pig stickers as Moray calls them—little use against dragons.

Cyril Côté now emerges from the forest. He is out of breath and sweating in the heat of the Triassic climate. He tells his story in a strained voice punctuated by gasps. The horror of it has not left him. The others will now share his horror and grief at the terrible demise of Lyon and Mathieu. Côté describes how he followed the trail of blood to the site of the massacre. How, stunned, he turned to run from the scene but was trapped by the dragon.

"It was horrible! It had a face like a snapping turtle, a long body covered with spines…and the tail…that ended in sharp barbs like a battle mace. It just looked at me for the longest time. I couldn't move…dared not move. I thought I was about to die. I prayed to Saint Michel to protect me. The dragon kept standing there, just staring at me. Trying to decide whether to eat me, I suppose. Finally, it turned and left. I ran it the opposite direction. Lost. But then I gained the ridge again and followed it back. I am ashamed of my cowardness. I could not fight the thing although it slew our comrades. But I am alive."

Jean-Michel Lesauvage, ever the conscientious commander, directs the group to begin a march, partly to put more distance between themselves and the dragons and partly to search for water. McGinley is concerned that they will be far from the whirlwind if it reappears, but he agrees they need water if they are to survive in the heat. They head west (maybe it's west), away from the plane and the ridge and the basin, through a thinning forest where bird-like things that are not exactly birds flit from tree to tree, following their progress.

"If I had my bow," says Abel, "we could have one of those things for lunch."

"They might be thinking of having *us* for lunch," says Duchamp.

"Monsieur Moray," says Mary as they make their way through the brush, "is it true that you Templars found the Holy Grail? You hid it away to guard it for future times when Muslims will be gone from the world?"

"If I told you that," says Moray, "I'd have to kill you."

There is a break in the trees up ahead. They can see bright sunlight reflecting from the surface of a vast body of water. They hurry toward this, gaining the bank of the inland sea which, although swampy, can be walked on. Off in the distance, in deeper water, there are giants: long-necked Brachiosaurus or his cousins, having a bath. In the sky above circle pterosaurs, gliding the air currents on membranous wings. McGinley's nonexistent dinosaur manual would identify the largest of these as quetzalcoatius northropi, named by future scientists for the feathered serpent deity of Mesoamerican myth. So far afield, none of these creatures discourage the time travelers from approaching the edge of the sea. Will it be brackish? Or can they drink?

Duchamp is the first to reach water's edge. He stoops to drink. "It is fresh!" he declares. He tosses off his armor; for him is has been like living inside a steam kettle. He wades into the water, oblivious to Lesauvage's admonishments not to. He is about waist deep when something grabs him from beneath the surface. It pulls him down, then, with the soldier clamped tightly in its jaws, it rolls and thrashes, sending waves of red-tinted water in all directions.

"A Crocodile!" cries Abel. "But look at the size of that thing!"

They retreat back to the woods. Following the line of the sea along the edge of the woods they come upon a fresh-water stream that is feeding the larger body of water. They drink. Abel fills his helmet with water and they walk into the woods again, now following the stream. For hours they walk, exhausted but fearful of stopping. So far they have not been accosted by dragons, birds, or insects. So far.

Ahead is another clearing. In the center of this is a shape that is familiar only to the travelers from the 19th and 20th centuries. It is a steam locomotive of an early type with several passenger cars attacked. This is remarkable enough but as they near the train they see that it is semi-transparent, as if it were only partly real. An illusion?

"How in the world did this get here?" asks Natsumi.

"I suspect it came the same way we did," answers McGinley, "thrown here by the space-time whirlwind."

"This is fantastic," says Lesauvage. "What is this thing?"

"Another enchantment from the witch," says Moray, nodding toward Natsumi.

"But look, you can see through it. It is like being in a dream," says Mary.

"I think," McGinley now offers, "that the locomotive and its cars did come here via the whirlwind, but somehow they are only partly in this time frame and partly in another. If true, it suggests an intriguing possibility."

"We go into the coach in this world, and go out the other side into another," says Natsumi. McGinley nods.

"None of this is happening," says Abel. "I had too much to drink last night. I'm still asleep and having a nightmare."

On closer examination they discover that the train and cars are sitting on rails attached to a circular platform. McGinley suggests this is a turntable of the type used in railyards to swing the locomotives around from one set of rails to another. They peer through the windows of the nearest coach and they think they can see more trains and box cars and maybe buildings on the other side—although so faintly they cannot be sure.

"Well," McGinley says, "we have two possible futures. We can stay here and maybe be eaten by dragons, or we can climb aboard the time-traveling train and see where it takes us. Please translate this for the Frenchmen, would you please, Mary?"

There is a dialogue now between Mary and the French soldiers and the Templar leader. The word, "merde" can be heard periodically. Lesauvage and Abel do not want to enter the strange translucent thing which sits here and which has begun to shimmer. Moray does not want to be wherever the soldiers are but still is a bit wary of the notion of leaping into another time.

McGinley notices the slight shimmer and realizes that once again, time is of the essence. He says nothing but pulls Natsumi along with him as he climbs the stairs to the passenger coach. Mary follows. Moray, now faced with a decision that will change the rest of his life one way or another, also follows. The train's shimmering now has a pulsating steady rhythm and the turntable has began to rotate. The soldiers watch in disbelief as the locomotive and cars disappear.

THE LAST SYLLABLE OF TIME

Ríona missed her parents, Colum and Muirgel Ó Brádaigh, and her younger sister, Caitríona, who they called "Cat." She worried that they might have fallen into the hands of the Others either during or after the raid on the beach. The Others had suffered awfully from the ravages of the plague and their few survivors had blamed Ríona's people for that suffering, as illogical and improbable as that might have been. Thus the raid. True, Ríona's people, the free-living folk that Riordan Ó Ciardha thought of as "Gypsies" were immune to the disease, but they were not the carriers who had infected the Others; that dubious honor belonged to Riordan, his alchemist master, Lorcan Mac Conmara, and the now gone-but-not-forgotten mad scientist, Nikolai Borisov.

Escaping the raid and discovering the abandoned time machine in the mountain's foothills, Mac Conmara had gotten the machine going and had set its coordinates to travel back through the singularity known as the Big Bang, out the other side, and into the parallel universe from which the time travelers had come. "You must make your decision," he had told his young apprentice. "Stay on this planet with your newly found love in her home or come with me back to County Cork where we belong."

The young lovers could not part from each other. As the countdown neared its final moments, Riordan and Ríona made their decision: they would accompany the alchemist and brave the dangers that might possibly await them on their journey through space-time. Now, as Ríona thought of her family, she had second thoughts. She watched through the transparent walls of the time machine as myriad stars rushed by like specks of dust in a windstorm. She had no notion of the immense distances and countless eons that shrank into a dense singularity, imploded, then expanded as a mirrored image of her own universe. There was only the ominous feeling that time itself had ceased to exist and that she hung immobile in a vast nothingness. Only tears and regret were still real for her.

"Ríona," said Riordan, "when we reach Ireland all the terror will be over. Once again we can be happy and enjoy life and the fruits of our own labor. I'll take you down to the village where I grew up and you can meet my father and mother."

"Perhaps," said Mac Conmara. "It is not a certainty that this machine can pinpoint the time and place we desire. I'm just hoping to reach Earth and not end up on some cold, dead planet, or worse, plunge into a blazing star."

"That's very comforting. Can't you cast a horoscope or something? At least we could know of our fate."

"Not so easy with an expanding universe. The constellations we knew have not formed yet."

"What if…here is a sobering thought…what if the Big Bang is the junction not just of our universe and Ríona's, but of multiple universes. How do we know we have entered our own? There could be millions of possible realities."

"According to my calculations, we will find out in just about one hour and a half. That's assuming the faster-than-light drive is working correctly. Meanwhile you better see to Ríona. She seems a bit upset by all this transition through space-time."

Chicago, 1934. Mary Dorr walked down Hyde Park Boulevard to the bus stop with Mrs. Sheridan. They sat on the top deck for the short ride to the Century of Progress Fair grounds at 23rd Street. Then, from the Hall of Science they crossed the 16th street bridge and walked through the Court of States to the new Midway on Northerly Island. Mrs. Sheridan wanted to see the Oriental dancers at the Chinese Theater but it was not open yet, so they walked over to the Midget Village instead.

They passed by the Streets of Paris, the Belgium Village, the Old Heidelberg Inn where a beer garden operated (End of Prohibition Day was only just last December), the A&P Gypsy show where the "apotheosis of America's womanly pulchritude" was on display (Mrs. Sheridan hurried Mary past that), the Gorilla Village where not one but two living gorillas entertained spectators, the Palace of Living Wonders where Duke Mills had assembled a variety of human "freaks" like the ones in the recent movie called *Freaks*, and the penny arcades, shooting galleries, and novelty rides like the Cyclone, the Lindy Loop, and Bozo's Heyday.

At the Midget Village over sixty Little People lived and worked putting on shows for fair visitors. They were billed as "Lilliputians" and their company included acrobats, folk dancers, and a full orchestra. The houses and shops were scaled down to match the diminutive inhabitants. Mary and Mrs. Sheridan watched an acrobat no bigger than a child climb to the top of a pole to do hand stands and other dangerous tricks which brought gasps from the crowd.

"Do you want to go back to the Hall of Science and go on the Sky Ride?" Mary asked Mrs. Sheridan.

"Oh no, Dear," she replied. "I would be terrified of the height."

"Well, we could go in the hall and see the Transparent Man. He's made of plastic and they say you can see his heart beating and the blood surging though his veins."

Mrs. Sheridan just scrunched up her eyebrows at this suggestion. Mary was not sure whether the Transparent Man had *all* his parts, but she wanted to find out. But not this trip. Instead, they opted to walk out onto the Enchanted Island. This was situated at the southern end of the Northerly Island and not too far away.

The Enchanted Island was dedicated to the children of fair goers and the young at heart. In its center, from within a pretend ocean, rose a miniature mountain on which children could slide. There were coaches to ride through mysterious caverns and up and down hills dotted with wooden figures of storybook characters. There was a sandy beach, a petting zoo, and a marionette show by Tony Sarg. All in all, it was perfectly suitable for Mrs. Sheridan.

It was approaching dusk as they strolled along one of the many wooded paths on the Enchanted Island. They stopped for a moment to sit on a bench next to a larger-than-life figure of the Tin Woodsman from the Wizard of Oz. Mrs. Sheridan was clearly out of breath. Her young charge, Mary, was just a teenager and could have continued on into the evening, but Mrs. Sheridan, Mary's aunt, was at the upper end of her fifties. And she had seen plenty of the Chicago's Century of Progress Fair by now. Enough to write about in her journal. She was about to have something even more extraordinary to write about, however.

"What's that thing over there?" Mary asked. She pointed to a large spherical object that sat amidst a patch of brambles just up the hill from where they sat. It was black, so black it nearly disappeared unless you looked just a little past it. "Let's go see," she urged her aunt.

There were so many futuristic structures at the fair, like the House of Tomorrow and the giant Havoline thermometer, but nothing quite so…simple and elegant as this. Curiously, the exhibit seemed to be hidden away from the main path. Perhaps it was an air balloon that had crashed, Mary though to herself. There had been hot air balloon races last fall, but those had been held up north in Glenview. If she couldn't ogle the Transparent Man she could at least look at this thing up close.

Inside the time machine the time travelers watched the approach of the woman and the girl. "They are human, at least," said Riordan.

"But their clothing," Mac Conmara pointed out, "is not of our era. This is our Earth, though, of that I feel certain."

"Should we go out to meet them?" asked Ríona.

"Wait a bit and see how they react to the time machine," answered the alchemist.

Mary braved the tangle of weeds and bramble bush to move closer to the time machine. She touched its surface but withdrew her hand immediately—It was warm, almost hot! Then she noticed the door. There was an indented space on it that could be a handle. Should she try it? Auntie was calling to her to come back. "Right away, young lady! This minute, Mary!" That intolerable commanding was enough incentive to push Mary to manipulate the handle. The door slid sideways exposing the interior of the time machine.

"Oh my God!" Mary uttered.

"She speaks English," said Riordan. "This is not Ireland, but it might be England or America." Then, switching from his native Gaelic to English, he addressed the girl:

"Greetings. My name is Riordan. I'm from Ireland. What's yours and…where are we? What is the date?"

"I'm Mary. Hello. What is this building? It isn't on the brochure. What kind of an exhibit is it?"

"It is a ship. We landed here by mistake and I'd appreciate it if you'd tell me where we are…and when."

"Like an air balloon? Oh, I see. Well, you are on the Enchanted Island. It is Sunday, July 22nd."

"What year?"

"Why, 1934, of course.

Mrs. Sheridan did not think it was proper to engage in conversation with strangers, especially ones who appeared to be performers in this elaborate circus of a World's Fair. The older one, however, attracted her attention. His long gray hair and beard, his peasant clothing—probably all a costume for his role, just as the midgets had dressed in folk dress—yet there was something about the way he smiled…

Mary was taken by the obvious foreign aspects of these airship fliers: their accents, their clothing out of a long past era, their disorientation. They must be part of one of the exhibits. But not knowing the year! Well, she figured they must have crashed here and the shock of it impaired their memories. They needed help.

"You should go to the clinic and get medical help," she told Riordan. "It's on our way and as we are ready to leave the fair, we'll walk with you down there."

"We may as well go and see the sights," Riordan said to Mac Conmara in Gaelic. The alchemist nodded in agreement. "Come, Ríona," Riordan said to the girl. "I think you are about to be amazed."

The massive semicircular shape of the Electrical Group was the first building to amaze Ríona. She had never seen a building of that size nor architecture so shockingly clean, simple, and yet monumental. Its sculptural dioramas glowed as sodium vapor lighting came on with the beginnings of dusk. Lights in a myriad of colors seemed to lift the building up into the sky.

Just ahead was the Federal Building, a golden-domed rotunda hung from a triangle of towering silver pylons. As lights came on here the spindles of its supporting cables sparkled with reds and greens. Yet the three pylons were dwarfed by the north-most tower of the Sky Ride, over six hundred feet tall and connected to its twin nearly two-hundred feet away on the other side of the North Lagoon. Even against the evening sky Ríona could make out the silhouettes of the ride's rocket-shaped gondolas carrying people for the ultimate view of the fair and the great metropolis beyond. Occasionally an arcing spotlight caught one of the gondolas and it looked like a comet flashing across the cosmos.

"What is this place?" asked Ríona. "Who are these people?"

"It is what is called a World's Fair," answer Riordan. "Something like your fetes but on a larger scale. I believe this is the one held in Chicago in the 1930s. It was called 'A Century of Progress.' See, the buildings and the exhibits all celebrate scientific and cultural progress and seek to predict the future."

"This isn't a real city then."

"No. While we are here we should see some of the exhibits. Have you ever seen a movie? A motion picture that seems real but is just an illusion? I think it is one of the greatest inventions of all time."

"Can we?"

Mary asked what they were talking about, picking up on a few words she thought she understood like "pictiúir gluaisne."

"We want to see a movie," Riordan told her.

"According to the brochure," Mary said, "Spore's Spectaculum is showing a spectacular film called, 'Niagara, Spectacle of the Mighty Cataracts.' Does that sound like something you would enjoy?"

"Yes, I think that would be interesting. Where do we find this Spectaculum?"

"You really don't know much about the fair for being a part of it. Well, here…take my map. We have to go now. Don't forget to check in with the clinic. I'll worry about you."

In another part of town that same night, three people walked to a nearby theater, the Biograph, to see a movie that was showing there called *Manhattan Melodrama.* The movie starred Clark Gable, Myrna Loy, and William Powell. One of the group was a woman named Polly Hamilton. Polly was living just around the corner from the Biograph Theater where she shared a room with Anna Sage, the second of the three theater goers. Polly had run away from her home in Fargo, North Dakota as a teenager and had worked for Anna in the older woman's whore house in Gary, Indiana.

In Chicago, Polly had gotten a job as a waitress at the S & S Sandwich Shop on Wilson avenue. She had moved in with Anna Sage. After work she often frequented a bar on Wilson called the Barrel of Fun. There she met a man who called himself Jimmy Lawrence. She thought him quite handsome in a rugged and earthy way. They began to date. When Anna met Lawrence some days later, she thought she recognized him. He was, she thought, a dead ringer for the gangster, John Dillinger.

Anna Sage, who had once been known as Ana Cumpănas, and whose real name was Ana Ivanova Akalieva, was a Romanian immigrant threatened with deportation due to her role as a prostitute and madam. With her knowledge that Dillinger was dating her friend, she thought she saw a way out of her dilemma. She contacted the FBI to make a deal. She would lead the FBI to Dillinger. She became an informant for Sergeant Martin Zarkovich who worked closely with Melvin Purvis, the chief agent in charge of capturing, or eliminating Dillinger.

The man who was calling himself Lawrence was restless. He told Polly they should go to a movie and he also asked Anna to accompany them. Anna made some excuse to leave the apartment momentarily and called the FBI. She would wear an orange dress, she told them, to make it easier to identify their suspect. Once the trio were inside the Biograph, the FBI moved to the street in front of the theater. Melvin Purvis stood in the doorway waiting for the movie to end. He would signal the other agents when he saw Dillinger come out. Clarence Hurt, Charles Winstead, and Herman Hollis were ready to close in once the signal was given.

Meanwhile, Riordan, Ríona, and Mac Conmara were seated in the huge amphitheater of Spoor's Spectaculum, built to accommodate up to 1,200 spectators. The screen upon which the film was projected measured 63 by 38 feet and the film stock itself, instead of the usual 35-millimeter width was 63-millimeters wide. The producer, George K. Spoor, called this unique film technology "Natural Vision," and promoted it as having a depth and clarity that made the motion picture nearly three-dimensional.

Spoor had been an early pioneer in the motion picture business, back when Chicago preceded Hollywood as the center of production in the new art form of cinema. He and his partner, Gilbert M. Anderson, founded Peerless Film Manufacturing Company in 1907. Later they opened a production facility on Argyle Street called Essanay Studios. There they created one- and two-reelers starring, among others, Charlie Chaplin, Ben Turpin, Wallace Beery, Colleen Moore, Gloria Swanson, and Francis X. Bushman, all unknown at the time. Anderson himself starred in the Bronco Billy westerns produced in Chicago.

That small success had been twenty years ago. Spoor's current endeavor, Natural Vision, was doomed to failure. The 1,200 seats today held only 30 or so people. Only three of these were in awe of the image on the screen of the rushing gray water, swirling and bubbling in torrents that tumbled furiously over the edge of the great falls of Niagara. The film lasted only 18 minutes. The time travelers exited the Spectaculum amidst a crowd of grumbling patrons. Thirty-five cents for that?

"That was wonderful," said Ríona. "I really thought it was real for a few minutes. I had to look at my feet to see if the water was rising."

"Let's go back to the time machine now," said Mac Conmara. "I'll try to make it jump back to Ireland in our own time. This century is too modern for my tastes."

Meanwhile, back on North Clark street, at the Biograph Theater, *Manhattan Melodrama* was nearing its conclusion. William Powell had just resigned as governor revealing how he was helped in the election by his childhood friend, played by Clark Gable, whose sentence for murder he had then shamelessly commuted. In the final scene, Powell and Myrna Loy walked off to start a new life. The audience walked out of the theater underwhelmed by the film. But *Manhattan Melodrama* was about to get a boost in its popularity.

Melvin Purvis was waiting in the doorway to the Biograph. Earlier, the theater manager, thinking Purvis and his men were plotting to rob the theater, called the Chicago Police. A wave of badges and a request not to disturb the surveillance had sent the cops packing. Now, as the audience began to filter out of the theater, Purvis scanned crowd for the woman in the orange dress. When he saw her, he pushed a cigar into his mouth and lit it as the signal to his men that he had located Dillinger. Dillinger, however, noticed Purvis, recognized him immediately, and pushed through the crowd in a rush to escape.

Mac Conmara and his companions had reached and entered the time machine. The alchemist fumbled with the settings on the control panel, trying to make the minute adjustments necessary for the short jump in space-time to sixteenth century Ireland. He might have said "Hang on to your hats," if they had been wearing hats, instead he said, "This time, for sure!" He pulled the lever that activated the brief countdown to the transmigration. Five, four, three, two, one…

Dillinger raced into the alley next to the biograph, reaching into his pocket to take out his Colt 280 Automatic pistol. The pistol snagged on his clothing and he was unable to turn and fire on the FBI agents. Hollis, Winstead, and Hurt chased into the alley after Dillinger, firing at him wildly. Just a Hollis stopped to take more careful aim at the running criminal, a large black sphere materialized at the end of the alley. A door opened in the sphere and Dillinger, unable to alter his headlong rush, plummeted through the doorway and fell onto the floor of the time machine at Riordan's feet.

"Close the door," Riordan yelled to Mac Conmara. "I don't think we're in Ireland.".

The time machine disappeared as quickly as it had materialized. In all the confusion of the chase and rapid gunfight, it had not been noticed by people in the alley. Numerous shots were fired by the FBI agents. Three people collapsed bleeding on the dirty alley floor. Witnesses would dip their handkerchiefs into the blood for souvenirs. Two of those shot were female bystanders who had the misfortune to have been in the line of fire, Theresa Paulas and Etta Natalsky. They were rushed to Columbus Hospital. The third shooting victim was a middle-aged man. He had been struck four times. One bullet proved to be fatal, entering the back of his neck and lodging in his brain. The blood made immediate identification difficult, as the man carried no wallet or other papers. It was assumed that it was Dillinger. The gangster had reportedly undergone plastic surgery during his stay in Chicago, and this complicated matters considerably. Purvis and the other agents made the identification, but conspiracy theories soon surfaced.

Anna Sage, the woman who had worn the orange dress, was mischaracterized by the press as "the woman in red." Although she had cooperated with the special task force of the FBI and helped to bring Dillinger to justice, she was deported anyway.

A horned lizard watched from its hide-away beneath a jagged rock as a bullsnake slithered by too close for comfort. In the distance across the rock-strewn crater, a bobcat hurried toward the rim on its way home, a desert cottontail hanging from its jaws. There had been a light New Mexican rain the day before and now the denizens of the crater were emerging to eat, or to be eaten. Today the Steller's Jay and mountain bluebird would feast on the lady bugs that covered the brush in a glorious tapestry of gold against green.

Capulin Volcano's cinder cone, which rose 1,000 feet above the grassy plain, was estimated to be much younger than some of the other volcanos in the area, perhaps only 60,000 years young. It was dormant and unlikely to erupt, so visitors to the Raton/Clayton volcanic field often hiked the five-mile path to the rim and descended into the crater to explore and view the ancient lava tubes. As the bobcat scampered down the side of the cone a pale green DeSoto Airflow 4-door sedan made its way up the access road toward the parking lot near the rim. Its passengers were not interested in hiking.

Glen Caldwell and Toby Ennis had borrowed the sedan from Victor Schnabel who had a vacation home in Santa Fe and kept the streamlined "car of the future" stabled there for his use when he was in the Land of Enchantment. Schnabel was a studio head at Paramount and had sent Caldwell and Ennis on a scouting mission for a proposed production of an as-yet untitled science fiction film about a moon landing. The volcano was a national park, but that presented few problems for the movie mogul whose connections gained him access to almost anywhere he wanted to film. The only exception had been his desire to shoot a feature at the Radiation Laboratory on the U of C Berkeley campus—that had been squelched by the military.

Caldwell and Ennis left the DeSoto and clambered down the path into the crater, carrying a heavy tripod and a 16-millimeter Bell and Howell Filmo loaded with highspeed black and white film. They set up the tripod near the center of the crater, attached the camera, took a light meter reading, and began a panoramic sweep of the crater.

"Ya, this'll do nicely," said Ennis.

"We left the beer up in the car," said Caldwell. "It'll be all warm when we get back up there."

"What's that over there?" asked Ennis, noticing a dark round shape next to one of the collapsed lava tubes.

Before they reached it, the time machine had opened and Mac Conmara, Riordan, and Ríona had stepped out, their hands held high in the air. They were followed closely by Dillinger who had an ugly pistol pointed at their backs. Surprised by his surroundings, which might have been a crater on the moon, Dillinger stopped short. "Wait a minute," he said. "What is this place?"

"Good question," said Mac Conmara. "Perhaps those two gentlemen over there can enlighten us."

Caldwell and Ennis had also stopped short. Seeing the man brandishing the handgun they raised their own hands. Dillinger gestured for them to approach.

"Where are we?" Dillinger asked.

"You are at the bottom of the crater of the cinder cone of Capulin Volcano. You didn't know that?" said Ennis.

"Excuse me," said Mac Conmara to Ennis, "but could you tell us the date?"

"Of course. It is April 14."

"What year?"

"Why…1935, of course. Say, now it's your turn to answer questions. Who are you, how did you get here, and what is that contraption you just came out of?"

"I'll ask the questions," said Dillinger, waving his pistol at Ennis and Caldwell. "And yes, how did we get here? What is that thing, and how can it be next year already?"

"If you will lower that gun, I will try to explain," answered Mac Conmara. What followed was, as it usually was when the time travelers were trapped into revealing the truth of it, a nearly pointless effort at convincing a very incredulous audience that they had arrived in a time machine.

"Okay, okay," said Dillinger. "Have it your way. You're time travelers. And I'm Santa Claus. Now, you two," he said to Ennis and Caldwell, "is there a city or a town nearby? I need to get to a telephone."

"Well, Capulin is the closest. Ain't much there, though. You head up that path and then down the cinder cone…"

"You have a car?"

"We have a car."

"You will drive me there. Now. All of you come along, I don't want none of you runnin' to the cops. Don't particularly want to have to kill you either. Yet."

The Village of Capulin lay five miles south of the volcano as the Bullock's oriole flew. The DeSota rolled into the tiny town—its population was under 60—and stopped in front of a long adobe building, the largest structure in town. Dillinger had assumed it to be a bank, ripe for plucking, but it was a multiple dwelling, built to accommodate several related families. There was a post office in town, but no one seemed to be around. No one the criminal could rob. There was also no police station, to Dillinger's delight. He could leave his captives here with little fear of them reporting his whereabouts. Take the sedan and find a larger town

About 150 miles due east, in the center of the Oklahoma panhandle, was the slightly larger town of Guymon. Here more than 2,000 souls lived on the high plains struggling to farm wheat or to raise livestock. The last few years had seen a drought of unimaginable proportions, and all over the wide wild West conditions had been dreadful. Cattle had depleted the ancient grasses of the Great Plains and wind erosion had swept away much of the topsoil. Eastern states had seen rolling dust storms they called "black blizzards." These began to spread westward, across Kansas and Arkansas and now into Texas, Oklahoma, and New Mexico. Guymon was at the very center of what would come to be called the "Dust Bowl." And today they would see the worst storm yet, on a day forever after to be known as "Black Sunday."

Down on Main street in Guymon, Randy Ferguson was walking by the Texas County Courthouse, a four-story brick building which had been built only a few years ago in a Neoclassical style, and which represented to the residents of the county seat, pride of enterprise and prosperity. The prosperity, though, was diminishing just as the topsoil was going, going, gone with the wind. Randy had left for a pleasant walk on a sunny Sunday afternoon but now found himself enveloped in a gray haze that was all too familiar these days.

A dust storm was surely coming. Everything would be covered in dust; it would get into their houses, coat their autos, spoil their food. They would eat dust, sleep in dust, breath in the caustic stuff that would choke them and sicken them and drive them insane with its persistence. Just another day in the euphoric West, thought Randy. Randy, like everyone in town, was beginning to accept the inevitability of the dust. But today was different.

Randy turned to look up at the Texas County Courthouse. The sky had turned black above it. Off in the plains to the northeast a great cloud was forming, like a fluffy cumulus cloud only this one was so dark and black it sucked the color out of everything. The cloud rolled toward town like an ocean wave, angry and dominating. Birds fell out of the sky before its onslaught. Small animals suffocated as it touched ground and pushed the clean air away. It crept forward, slowly swallowing buildings and vehicles. It was leaving behind ton upon ton of the dreaded dust.

As the storm neared Capulin, New Mexico, the wind had picked up. It stabbed at the town. Dillinger had lined the time travelers and the movie people up against the adobe building, getting ready to make his exit. The darkness grew quickly as the first gusts brought the stinging dust. Within minutes visibility was only a few feet. Dillinger felt for the car which now was impossible to see in the crepuscular murk. He staggered and fell. The others felt for a door into the building. Riordan grabbed Ríona's hand.

The dust cloud had poured over the top of the building and swirled back up from the ground striking their faces and bodies like hundreds of tiny fists. They could not breathe. At last a door opened and someone called from inside the adobe: "Aqui! Rápido!" Now they all managed to join hands. Ennis was closest to the open door and pulled the rest after him, a human chain of desperation. Finally inside the adobe, they were safe. For a time.

"Buenos tardes," said the voice. A small head peeked out from around the side of an old upholstered armchair. "Me llamo es José. Mi madre no está en casa. Pero bienvenida."

José was a young boy of eight or nine with uncombed hair, no shirt, and a red bandana tied at his neck, cowboy-wise. He came all the way out from behind the chair and smiled. One of his front teeth was missing.

"Hablo usted Inglés?" asked Riordan.

"Un poco…a little," the young boy answered.

"How is it you know Spanish?" Mac Conmara asked Riordan.

"I don't. Just that much." Then to José he said, "Muchas gracias, José. We got caught in that storm. You may have saved our lives."

"Da nada. And the bad hombre with the pistola, is he muerta?"

"Oh!" said Riordan. "We forgot about him. Did he make it into the car, do you think?"

"Why worry about that asshole?" said Ennis.

"Well, he could have shot us, but he didn't. Everybody's life is worth something."

"You know who that was, don't you?" Ennis said. "That was John Dillinger. Public enemy number one."

"Dillinger," said Riordan. 'I've read about him. Wasn't he killed at a movie theater…oh! I guess we just changed history. That's not a good thing."

"No, it isn't," said Mac Conmara. "However, if the storm took care of him…"

"Maybe things won't change all that much."

"That is one hell of a dust storm out there," said Caldwell. "Where are your parents, young man?"

"My momma is in Des Moines at the market. I don't have no poppa. Mi abuela is next door. She looks after me. That really was John Dillinger? El Rey Proscrito?"

"The very same. Vicious criminal, they say. Pretty famous."

The men and the boy had slept on the floor of José's casa on an old Mexican horse blanket that served as a rug. Ríona had curled up in José's bed which he had graciously offered to her. When she awoke, José was already in the kitchen making noise with the pots and pans. The others snored and twitched on the rug.

"José," she said, "let me help you with that."

"It's okay. Senorita," said José. "I'm good at the coffee and tortillas. I do this a lot. I got some beans to warm up and then we're ready."

There was a frying pan simmering on one of the stove's burners that contained a red liquid which the boy stirred. "A little water, garlic, and some good red chile from Chimayo," he explained. "You like hot or mild?"

Mac Conmra had awakened and gone to the window to peer out into the gloom. He expected to see the slumped corpse of the criminal covered in dust, perhaps a hand stretched out and grasping for the car door. Only the car was gone and Dillinger with it. How far had he gotten in that storm, the alchemist wondered? Ennis joined him at the window.

"Damnit!" said Ennis. "That bastard's stolen our car! Now we're stranded."

"Well," said Mac Conmara, "maybe we can give you a lift."

Five of them in the time machine made for cramped quarters. Mac Conmara had used the remote to bring the sphere to them so that they hadn't needed to climb up the volcano to get to it. José had been fascinated by the contraption and dearly wanted to take a ride in it, but Mac Conmara had vetoed that notion. Ríona was whispering in Riordan's ear about how much she missed her home and her family. So far, she had been to a futuristic fair, an extinct volcano, had been threatened at gunpoint, and had been battered by a onslaught of dust whose shear volume could have constructed its own planet.

"Say," said Ennis, "could you fly this thing low over the ground like a biplane? We could look for that thieving bastard. He couldn't have gone far."

"Better than that," answered the alchemist. "Use the viewing console to search the area." He showed Ennis how to operate the device using its joystick to change focus and direction.

"Ríona wants to go home," Riordan told Mac Conmara. "She isn't cut out for jumping through time like we are. I'll stay with her on her planet, that is, if you can get us back there."

Before Mac Conmara could answer, Ennis yelled, "Eureka! I found the DeSoto. Can't be more than one of them in these parts. It's sitting in front of a bank in some small town."

"Read me the coordinates," said the alchemist. "I'll add a point or two so we don't land right on top of the car or in the city street. There should be four coordinates."

The time machine settled gently down on top of a high bluff overlooking the town. The time travelers left the machine to look at the spectacular New Mexican landscape that spread out in all directions around them. On the side of the bluff facing the town was a sign, a row of large letters cut out of wood, not unlike the ones in California that spelled Hollywoodland. Only these spelled N O T A R.

"Notar?" said Riordan. "What do you suppose that means?"

"It's the name of the town," answered Mac Conmara. "Only, see how the N and the R are backwards? This is Raton, wherever that is."

"It is a small New Mexican town on the border with Colorado," said Caldwell. "The earliest Santa Fe Trail came over the pass here, but only mules and donkeys could negotiate it safely. Originally, the campsite here was called Willow Springs. The railroad first came over the pass in the late 1870s."

"Wait a minute," said Ennis, "how do you know so much about this place? You've never been here."

"No, but I can read. See, I found this tourist handout in the trash can over there. It's a wealth of information. There's a map of historic buildings. The one our car is parked in front of is probably the Raton Bank Building. The hill we are on is called Goat Hill. We can climb down the access road to get to town."

Which they did. They walked up First street, past the Raton Railroad Station, the Atchison, Topeka and Santa Fe Reading Room, and the Wells Fargo Express building. Raton had the look of a nineteenth century town with typical two-story brick buildings sporting decorative façades. Only the train station smacked of Southwestern design. Something was a little off, however. Automobiles parked on the streets looked a bit too modern for the 1930s. And a sign on the train station identified it as an Amtrak depot.

"Master," Riordan said to Mac Conmara, "I don't think we're in 1935 anymore."

Ennis and Caldwell spotted the DeSoto and took off in a run down the street. The others followed more slowly. When the movie people got to the car they found it locked.

"Damn!," said Ennis. "I guess we'll have to break a window." He looked around for a rock and found a discarded brick in the alley next to the bank building. He picked it up and returned to the car, ready to smash a window, but then thought about what their boss might say. "Old man Schnabel will have our heads when he finds out we fucked up his favorite car."

"Ya, but if we don't get it back…" said Caldwell.

Ennis hefted the brick and took aim at a side window. The men hadn't noticed the modern cars on the street, nor had they noticed the two police officers who were watching them as they tried to steal back the DeSoto. Officer Robert "Bud" Brooks and Officer Pete Peterson, seasoned men in blue, were alert and ready for action.

"Hey you," yelled Officer Brooks, "what do you think you're doing? That's the mayor's car, you fool. Better drop that brick!"

Ennis did so and turned to confront the policeman. "Mayor? Mayor who? This is our car…or at least, it's our boss's car. It was stolen from us yesterday by John Dillinger. What did he do, sell your mayor our car?"

"John Dillinger? Say…what are you trying to pull? Dillinger was killed over twenty years ago. And Mayor James Lawrence has owned that car for at least that long."

Office Peterson now joined in: "It's a classic. The mayor was driving it when he first came to town…during that horrible dust storm all those years ago. He's a sort of local hero, stopping those bank robbers that very day. But you wouldn't know any of that, being outsiders. We don't like outsiders much around here. We only like 'em when they leave town. You get it?"

"Now wait a minute," complained Caldwell. "The car is registered to Victor Schnabel. The papers are in the glove compartment. Get your mayor to open it up and let's see who's right and who isn't."

"I've a better idea, boys. You can come down to the station house with us and wait in a nice cozy jail cell while we see if the mayor wants to press charges."

Mac Conmara, Riordan, and Ríona had been exploring the windows of the gift shops and other stores along the street, taking their time catching up with Ennis and Caldwell. When they got to where the DeSoto was parked, they saw their companions being led away by the two policemen. They followed, but not too closely. Something was amiss and they did not wish to make things more complicated until they understood what was happening.

They waited outside the police station for Ennis and Caldwell to come back out, figuring that they were just reporting the stolen car. But after many minutes had elapsed and the pair had not emerged, they decided to enter the building. A man sat behind a desk in the front room, smoking a cigarette and reading a magazine. Mac Conmara spoke to him:

"We saw our friends come in here with two policemen. Can you tell us where they are and what is happening to them? We may be able to help."

"Oh? You friends of them would-be car thieves? You wanna get arrested too?"

"I don't know what you mean. There must be some misunderstanding. Their car was stolen from them yesterday. They were trying to get it back. We can vouch for them."

"You see that picture on the wall over there?" The man pointed to a framed portrait. "That's Mayor Lawrence. That was his car they were trying to steal. Still want to vouch for them?"

They looked at the portrait. It was a glossy color photograph of a good-looking older man with graying hair wearing a pin-striped suit and a wide tie decorated with blue paisleys.

"He's a bit older in that photograph," said Max Conmara, "but that's Dillinger."

They had retreated to the top of Goat Hill and had sat in the shade under a cottonwood tree next to the time machine. Ríona leaned against Riordan, a despondent look on her face. Riordan smiled at her;

it seemed to help a little. The alchemist suddenly stood up and looked out over the wooden sign letters at the town below.

"Well, as I see it, we've got two problems," said Mac Conmara.

"Only two?" asked Riordan.

"One," continued the alchemist, "is that our friends need to be sprung from jail and returned to their own time. With their automobile if possible."

"And two?

"And two, there is Dillinger. He shouldn't be here. Actually, he should not be anywhere."

"But, although we sort of changed history, it looks like the man reformed. He stopped a bank robbery, became a local hero, and eventually was elected mayor of the town. They seem to like him."

"Certainly history didn't change the way it would have if Dillinger had remained in Chicago and not been killed. Maybe there were no abrupt changes to history because he was effectively removed from that space-time. Remember when Wayland and Judo went back and killed Hitler? That was considerably different."

"There is a third problem," said Riordan. "Ríona wants to go home."

"I don't like this world so much," Ríona said. "I miss my family and my friends."

"Even though your world is half dead from the plague?" said Riordan, and immediately regretted saying it.

"One thing at a time," said Mac Conmara. "First, how do we rescue the movie people?"

"When we were on the scientist Borisov's planet, Professor McGinley made time bubbles we could walk around in, unseen because we were shifted out of time just enough."

"Yes, but he used the Dweller's apparatus to do that. This machine isn't capable of that."

"Could we hop back in time just before the police grab our friends?"

"Altering history again. Even a little, I think is risky."

"Why don't you appeal to that mayor…Dillinger?" said Ríona.

"Appeal? Why don't we confront him. Tell him we'll send him back through time to that alley in Chicago?"

"Hm, Riordan, I think you…and you, Ríona…have the germ of a plan there. Being nice or being nasty to Dillinger…that may be the key." Mac Conmara clapped his hands together. "Yes, indeed. The key!"

John Dillinger, overcome by the plummeting dust, had fallen to the ground gasping for breath. He flailed his hands and by chance his left hand encountered the side of the DeSoto. Blinded by the dust, he felt for the door handle, found it, and pulled himself up. He managed to swing the door open against the strong wind and to climb into the car. He sat there, stunned for a time, then wiped the dust from his eyes with a handkerchief he had worn in his suitcoat pocket. Time to evaluate his situation.

He had the car, he had his handgun, he no longer had hostages, he was stranded out in some miserable little town in New Mexico…of all places…but he was alive and kicking. He could wait out the storm and then drive off into the sunset. They had great sunsets here, didn't they? And banks.

John Dillinger was a bank robber of renown. He had robbed upwards of 24 banks in his career—so far. He had been in and out of jail and had escaped several times, most dramatically in March of 1934 from an escape-proof jail in Crown Point, Indiana, using a fake gun he had carved from a piece of wood and painted black. He had shot it out with Federal agents at a vacation lodge called Little Bohemia in Manitowish Waters, Wisconsin, and escaped uninjured. He had undergone plastic surgery but it had failed to significantly alter his appearance.

Dusk brought an end to the dust storm. Dillinger had napped, gotten out of the car to relieve himself against the adobe building, thumbed his nose at the town, and then had driven off along Highway 67 toward the north. There hadn't been a sunset, or if there had, it had been hidden in the gloom. At Raton he parked the DeSoto on the street a few blocks from the Raton Bank and Trust which he had located practically by instinct. He would wait until morning when the bank opened and make a withdrawal—his way.

Morning: saffron to gold to rose as a weary sunrise filtered through the last filaments of wind-blow dust. An unkindness of ravens roosting atop a dental façade heralded daybreak with kraas and croaks. A banker prompt with his key in the lock made a clack to add to the cacophony. Dillinger was awake. Dillinger saw the banker enter, draw up the faded green shade, turn over the closed/open sign. He checked the clip of the Colt 280: locked and loaded, a cartridge in the chamber. He flipped off the safety. Slowly he made his way down the sidewalk toward the bank building. He wasn't the first customer of the day, however.

Dillinger entered the bank and stopped short. Two men were at the cashier's cage. They wore denim shirts with metal buttons, wide-brimmed straw hats, and bandanas which they had tied above their noses to hide their features. A red bandana and a green bandana. A revolver in red bandana's hand. A shotgun, looking more ancient than the dust that had covered the town, held by green bandana. Fucking cowboys, thought Dillinger. They had forced the bank teller to fill a cloth bag with money. They turned. Dillinger was aiming his own weapon at them.

"Hold it right there, amigos," said Dillinger. "Let's have that money bag."

The teller, being no fool, had handed over the money, but at the same time, had pushed the silent alarm button with his knee. The police chief, one Jesus Morales, had just finished a breakfast burrito at Marie's Café, and had returned to his cruiser when the call came over his car radio. He arrived at the scene of the crime to see Dillinger holding off the two bank robbers. Chief Morales added his own firepower to Dillinger's.

"Nice work," Morales said. "I'll take it from here."

Dillinger, identifying himself once again as James Lawrence, received a commendation from the Raton City Council and a nominal reward from the bank. It was the beginning of his new life as an upstanding citizen. Graft, he soon learned, was just as profitable as armed robbery, and much safer. He was invited to speak about his heroic capture of the bank robbers at the local Rotary Club on the following week. There he made new friends: businessmen with whom he sensed a shared love of easy money and a lack of scruples. He invested his reward money in a partnership in a proposed bowling alley. The bank approved a loan for his venture although he had no collateral. A kickback to the bank's president had assured the funding.

The rest was history—history that would not have taken place if Dillinger had been killed in the alley next to the Biograph. Now he was the mayor of the small New Mexican town of Raton. The kickbacks came his way. The contracts went to the biggest donners. Life was good. Life could be celebrated with a fiesta now and then. Now there was a grand pig roast underway at Roundhouse Memorial Park. Mayor

"Jimmy" Lawrence was on hand to give a short speech on the subject of the importance of commercial development to the region and to shake a few hands.

The park was on the site of the old railroad roundhouse and still had remnants of the old tracks. People from town mingled with ranchers from all around the county displaying a diverse array of Western straw hats with hat bands ranging from plain to beaded to elaborately crafted turquoise and silver. A string band played "Entriega de Novios" (March of the Newlyweds), as a wedding party danced, the bride in flowing white skirts, the groom in Spanish Colonial costume. Children ran laughing and shouting around a wooden gazebo next to where the band was playing. Three-hundred pounds of sizzling swine turned slowly on a spit over an open fire.

Mayor Lawrence strutted from his classic DeSoto Airflow 4-door sedan over the scruffy grass to the gazebo with his entourage of two bodyguards, large men with closely cropped hair and malevolent countenances, and his newly appointed police chief, a man named Horace Kilby, with spit-shined shoes, brilliant silver badge, crisply ironed khakis, and a well-oiled sidearm prominently displayed.. Sort oflike the old days of the Dillinger gang, yet not like the old days when cops were out to get them. Now the mayor controlled the cops. Cops that chased troublemakers out of town, often beating some sense into them before their exit. Lawrence was the Law and Order mayor of Raton. His police force, not reflecting the majority Hispanic population of the region, was one of the least diverse in the Land of Enchantment.

Lawrence was not beloved of the people. There were the Haves and the Have-nots, and the Haves got richer while the Have-nots got poorer. Lawrence was all about the economy. Lawrence was, however, skittish of the Have-nots—hence the bodyguards. Have-nots had a tendency to confront him when he appeared in public. And these days, he couldn't just back them down with a wave of a pistol, like in the old days. But his police force could.

In many cities in the United State during that time, the Civil Rights movement was gaining momentum. In two years from now, the historic March on Washington would take place and Doctor Martin Luther King Junior would give his famous "I have a dream" speech. In New Mexico, there was civil unrest among Hispanics, fueled in part by an activist named Reies Lopez Tijerina.

Tijerina, during a trip to Mexico, had learned about the Treaty of Guadalupe Hidalgo which guaranteed land grants to descendants of the original Spanish land grantees when most of the southwestern portion of the United states was part of Spain. Land thereafter grabbed by powerful Anglos. Regaining those rights was a cause Tijerina took up. He founded a religious community in Arizona called the Valley of Peace bit soon found himself in conflict with local government. After several run-ins with the law in which he was accused of theft and other misdemeanors, Tijerina became a fugitive.

Tijerina and some of the families from the Valley of Peace hid out for a while in the ghost town of Gobernagor, New Mexico. By 1958 he had become an activist. Speaking in Chama, New Mexico, to a group of land grant heirs about the Treaty of Guadalupe Hidalgo, the U.S. Constitution, and the suppression of their rights, he was attacked and clubbed in the head. This contributed to his growing popularity with many Hispanos. He began organizing strikes. In 1963, the year of the March on Washington, Reies Lopez Tijerina and Eduardo Chávez created Alianza of Pueblos and Pobladores, Alliance of Towns and Settlers, or simply, La Alianza. The press nicknamed him, "Don Quixote," or sometimes, "King Tiger."

Now Mayor Jimmy Lawrence, aka John Dillinger, mounted the platform under the gazebo at Roundhouse Memorial Park. Just as he uttered his introduction: "Friends…" the large crowd surrounding the venue began voicing various phrases in Spanish which, of course, Dillinger did not understand, not having taken it upon himself in the last twenty years of living in the Southwest to learn the language. Someone shouted: "Vivan los pueblos republicans libres de Nuevo Mexico!" One of the Anglo ranchers on the outskirts of the crowd countered with, "Communists! Agitators!" Dillinger backed away, sensing an impending skirmish. His bodyguards rushed him off the platform and headed for the DeSoto with Dillinger in tow. The time machine materialized next to the classic auto just before they reached it.

The door opened; Dillinger tried to stop his forward momentum, but once again, he ended up inside the time machine. This time he knew where he was and he did not like it. The door closed preventing the two bodyguards from following the mayor inside. They banged futilely on the door. Dillinger fumbled with his jacket pocket, but he had not been carrying a weapon today. A foolish mistake, perhaps.

"Hello, Mr. Dillinger," said Mac Conmara. "Welcome to oblivion."

"You can't keep me here," shouted Dillinger. "My bodyguards…"

"Look outside. What do you see?"

What he saw was a snow-covered landscape. Polar bears patrolled the edges of ice floes off a nearby shore.

"Welcome to the North Pole," said Mac Conmara. "Would you like to get out now?"

Perhaps Dillinger's body language indicated that he was about to rush the alchemist. Perhaps the alchemist's apprentice was just cautious and anticipated resistance. Riordan threw a body block against the gangster, knocking him to the floor. He was about to follow this up with a good swift kick but Mac Conmara stopped him.

No response. Dillinger just glared back at the alchemist. He started to get to his feet, but Riordan pushed him back down.

"I could also simply take you back in time to that alley where FBI agents will shoot you dead. Or you can go back to New Mexico, release our friends, give them the keys to the automobile, and go about your own business as usual. What is your answer? I hate to have to open the door and let all that cold air in."

Dillinger reluctantly nodded in the affirmative. Mac Conmara made some adjustments to the control panel and instantly the time machine appeared once again in the lot next to the DeSoto. The two bodyguards were still standing there, dumbfounded. Seeing them through the transparent walls of the machine, the alchemist made one more slight adjustment and the time machine skipped forward in time about an hour. Now the bodyguards were gone.

"Please understand," said Mac Conmara, "that I can snatch you from anywhere you happen to be. I've entered your essential elements into the time machine's database. It can find you and scoop you up like a fish in a meadow stream." This was all nonsense, of course, but Dillinger did not know that. "Now go do as we have instructed, and no tricks…we'll be watching."

They did watch as Dillinger drove the DeSoto straight to the police station. After an agonizing twenty minutes, during which the time travelers worried that they had underestimated the gangster, Ennis and Caldwell emerged from the police station, got into the DeSoto, and drove away. None of the three time travelers knew what a high-five was, but they celebrated their successful rescue with appropriate jubilance.

"Twenty years have passed since those men and the car disappeared," said Riordan. "What do you think they'll do now?"

"That's anybody's guess. We could return them to their own time, but the car would remain here. It is an interesting dilemma. We've done the best we can."

"What will happen to Dillinger?"

"If he doesn't behave himself there are some angry people out there that may very well see that he gets his comeuppance So now it is your turn…yours and Ríona's. Do you still want to go back, Ríona?"

Ríona seemed to consider, which heartened Riordan, as he had believed she was insistent upon the return journey. Maybe she was changing her mind? Before she could answer, however…

Things were happening in the Land of Enchantment. Glen Caldwell and Toby Ennis were surprised when the sheriff opened their cell door and handed them the keys to the DeSoto. He said, "Get the hell out of town." They hurried to the car, gave a last look around just in case this was some kind of trick, then got in the DeSoto and drove off.

"Bet that alchemist fellow had something to do with this," said Ennis. Caldwell nodded and voiced an affirming "Yup."

They headed north towards Trinidad, Colorado, the DeSoto struggling with the gain in altitude as they negotiated the pass. To the east, Barlett Mesa dominated the landscape. Ahead, Fisher's Peak rose nearly 10,000 feet to mark the edge of Colorado. Pinyon and juniper dotted the low foothills while higher up on the mesa they could glimpse stands of Douglas fir and quaking aspen. The road followed Raton Creek and the Amtrak route, rails once used by the Atchison, Topeka and Santa Fe Railway. Just before a small cluster of houses with the appropriate name of Starkville, the makeshift timer clicked its last click.

Dillinger had ordered his bodyguards to place two sticks of dynamite and a blasting cap under the hood of the DeSoto, connecting this dire device to the car battery through a circuit controlled by an old alarm clock. He was genuinely sorry to see the car destroyed, but principles were principles. The resulting fireball could be seen as far north as Trinidad.

Ríona was considering her answer to the question about returning all those millions of light years to her home planet. Braving the transition through the singularity that they called the Big Bang—the beginnings of this universe and the endings of her own. She would be encountering the ravages of plague which had nearly annihilated half the planet—were her people still immune? Had the roving gangs of the Others disrupted her people's tranquil lives. Indeed, had her people been killed by the jealous survivors of the Others? And, most importantly, would Riordan stay with her? Before she could answer, however…

Sheriff Horace Kilby, Officer Robert "Bud" Brooks, and Officer Pete Peterson, under the direction of Mayor James Lawrence himself, sprang up in a circle around the time machine which was still standing in the parking lot of the Roundhouse Memorial Park. Automatic weapons were aimed at the large dark sphere. Riordan happened to see the attackers before they could fire and yelled a warning at Mac Conmara. The alchemist began fiddling with the buttons and dials and levers on the control panel,

Bullets like angry hornets flew at the time machine. They bounced harmlessly to the ground. Undaunted. Dillinger summoned his bodyguards. They brought forth an army surplus bazooka, dropped in a very lethal shell, and lowered the weapon point blank at the time machine. All Riordan could say was, "Oh, shit!"

The weapon was fired, the shell struck the time machine just at the instant that Mac Conmara activated the transformation sequence. The sphere leaped through space-time carrying the shell, still unexploded, along with it. What the alchemist intended to be another short jump, just a little jiggle through space-time, turned out to be…

Byron Grush

The Roundhouse at the Edge of Eternity

Dr. Madison James McGinley of the Radiation Lab in Oakridge, Tennessee, his neighbor Natsumi Ito, Mary Wollstonecraft who is the future Mary Shelley, and Jacques de Moray, Grand Master of the Knights Templar are seated in a railroad passenger car of early nineteenth century design which is connected to a Tiger Class LDCR locomotive called the Lethe. The Lethe is named after one of the five rivers of the Hades underworld of Greek mythology (which may or may not be significant). The Lethe sits on a turntable which services a railyard roundhouse, a semicircular brick building with 27 stalls for storing locomotives. Dark smoke rises from several vents in the roof of the roundhouse.

It might be the roundhouse at Aurora, Illinois, for the Chicago, Burlington, and Quincy Railroad. Or it might be the East Broad Top Railroad and Coal Company's roundhouse at Rockhill Furnace, Pennsylvania. It might be the one at the Birmingham Curzon Street Station in England. Or at Werris Creek in New South Wales. Or at Chapleau, Ontario or Avignon, France or Budapest's North Depot or at Tsuyama or Guadalajara or Zurich or Barreiro or almost anywhere in the world where there are trains.

But it isn't anywhere in the world, at least not the world that Madison McGinley lives in. And this is not 1952 or 1815 or 1304, the years from which the aforementioned passengers have come. And yet, it is all those places and all those times, simultaneously. The roundhouse is perched, however precariously, on the edge of eternity, where time and space exist, or don't exist—or do and don't simultaneously.

McGinley and company look out the windows of the passenger car, each hoping for a view of home or at least, something familiar. But there are no buildings, no railyard with boxcars and hobos and stray dogs, no cityscape or a sky filled with airplanes—no people. There are only stars and more stars, swirling galaxies and space dust, black holes and nebulae with more colors than the rainbow can hold, and all this suspended in darkness so black and so immeasurable that the minds of these mere mortals cannot grasp its immensity. Endless and vast, it is simultaneously infinite and a single point of energy, a singularity which at any minute might explode to create another universe.

Maybe it had been a mistake to board the train. Maybe they should have stayed in the Triassic and taken their chances with hungry dinosaurs stalking them. One never knows what Mother Time has in store. Two of their number are still struggling with the concept of transmutation. Mary Wollstonecraft has thought it a hoax, although she is hard pressed to explain her recent experiences. Jacques de Moray is convinced it was enchantment and that Natsumi is the witch that had conjured it all up. Natsumi is relying on McGinley to rescue them and McGinley is dumbfounded, perplexed, adrift when it comes to solutions for this particular puzzlement.

McGinley understands much of the dynamics of the space-time continuum having traveled here and there and then by device or by accident. But this—this is timelessness, spacelessness, a void inside of a void. Well, at least there are stars out there. That is encouraging. When they had stood in the Mesozoic forest watching the unlikely vision of this train slowly shimmering as if it were slipping in and out of overlapping space-time frames, they had assumed it to be a portal, a door from there to another here—one without dinosaurs. But it is a door to nowhere. You couldn't get off the train at this or any other station.

There is movement. The passengers are jostled. The turntable is rotating. As it turns, the view out the window changes rapidly like a time-lapse movie. Scenes from the virtual movie flash by in a subliminal staccato: a city of cone-shaped buildings made of crystal, a garden of spider web trees dripping with blossoms that look like bleeding hearts, junkyards of rusting rocket ships and the marquees from drive-in movie theaters, circus tents in flames, sand dunes stretching endlessly toward a purple sunset, a village of cat-like creatures that snap at the train with needle-sharp teeth as it passes, a profusion of death's head moths that smother the windows blocking the view.

Then suddenly the train is moving. The engine makes I-think-I-can-I-think-I-can chugging sounds and the wheels clatter against the steel rails which, once the moths have left and the window view is clear again, appear to be suspended in space. A night sky filled with stars surrounds them. No landscape, no distant mountain range, no churning ocean…just empty space and a few stars for scale. McGinley makes a decision. This train must be heading somewhere. The flickering images they witnessed must mean that the train travels along space-time rifts. There has to be a station where they can disembark. He will talk to the engineer…there is one, isn't there?

McGinley moves to the door at the end of the car where it attaches to the locomotive and tender. The door opens easily and he sees that he must traverse a catwalk that is hung along the side of the engine so that he can obtain access to the engine's cab. One foot in front of the next along the narrow catwalk he goes, inch by inch, with empty space below him if he slips. His hands sweat as he clings to a wire railing and moves cautiously along the catwalk.

Now he is able to pull himself up and into the cab. There he sees the engineer, a rough-looking man of uncertain age (although it must be considerable), dressed in blue and white striped overalls (covered with grit and grime), a short-billed hat also striped blue and white, and a red bandana tied about his neck. The man notices McGinley but seems ambivalent to his presence. McGinley has to raise his voice to be heard above the noise of the engine.

Back in the passenger car the others are waiting. The blackness outside is offset by the flickering of gas light from the sconces on the walls of the car. It is hypnotic. Mary changes her position and slides across the green leather seat to be next to the Templar. "Come now, Monsieur de Moray, talk to me. I won't bite," she says.

"There is nothing to say," answers Moray. She is a 16-year-old girl and vivacious. He is a 70-year-old man and has taken a vow of celibacy. However, her attention to him has a certain charm—innocent charm?

"I tell you what, I'll tell you a secret and you tell me one," she says. "I'll start. I am having an affair with a married man. He is married to a woman who is my age and he is much older than she. He does not love her. He is a famous poet…well, maybe not so famous…yet. Do you think me horrible?"

"Jesus would not be happy with you. We Templars are Gnostics. We do not associate with women in that way. So I cannot advise you."

"Now you tell me a secret. Look out the window…there is nothing but empty space out there. We probably will die soon. So it is all right to tell me…tell me about the Holy Grail. Are you hiding it somewhere? Does it even exist?"

"What do you know about the Grail?"

"I am well read," she answers. "There is an epic poem by Eschenbach in which Parzival, a knight of King Arthur's round table seeks the Grail and finds it guarded by the Fisher King. The Fisher King has an army called the Templeise and they keep the Grail in a temple. Does that sound familiar?"

"This is not 'The Poor Fellow-Soldiers of Christ and of the Temple of Solomon,' as we call ourselves. And your poem is fiction, is it not?"

"Another writer, Roger of Boron, claimed that the Grail was in fact the cup Christ drank from and passed around at the Last Supper. 'This is my blood,' the Christ said. The same cup, tells Boron, was used by Joseph of Arimathea to save drops of the Christ's blood as he hung on the cross. Joseph took the cup to Avalon at Glastonbury. Perhaps the Templars found it there."

"There are those," comments Moray, "that say that the term 'grail' actually refers to the lineage of descent from Jesus Christ and Mary Magdalene. In the French 'san grail' is a pun on 'sang real'; holy grail means royal blood. So it is not a cup or a stone or a plate. Perhaps it is a manuscript, a missing book of the Bible which tells of this mystery. But I will not say that we Templars found this thing in the Temple of Solomon or have guarded it ever since."

"You won't tell me, but you don't deny it either. And what about that mummified severed head? There is something very intriguing about a severed head."

"This is a charge they use to discredit us. They say we worship the head of John the Baptist. Ridiculous. There is no such thing. And why would that be a sin if we had such a Holy object? Do not all the churches have their reliquaries, their châsses for the bones of saints, fragments of the True Cross, the skulls of popes?"

"Fascination with the dead. In my day we have institutions devoted to dissection and study of the human body. In Paris you have the famous morgue where people come to view suicides pulled from the

Seine. And the catacombs with hundreds of skulls and bones all staked up artistically," says Mary. Her own fascination with dead things surfaces unmistakably.

"I do not know of this morgue or these catacombs. But I have been on the battlefields amongst blood and gore that you would shy away from. It is the human condition to inflict suffering on others. This is why we fight: to end war."

"I wonder..."

McGinley's shouting eventually gets the attention of the engineer. The man turns and points to a stack of wood in the adjacent tender. "Grab a few sticks, will ye, me good fellow?" the engineer says. McGinley does so and he is directed to shove these into the open firebox that services the boiler. The heat is intense. He throws a log into the firebox and backs quickly away. The engineer laughs.

"Not much skill is necessary, boyo. But see thee do not get singed. I'm short of burn ointment."

"Sir," says McGinley, "could you tell me...where are we headed? There seems to be a lack of landscape to view." He hesitates to point out that they seem to be in outer space.

"Depends on the signals. Green we go east, red we go west. What does yer ticket tell ye? What station be ye headed fer?"

"We were sort of hoping, somewhere on Earth. Any century would probably do."

"Ah yes, there's that. I canna do naught else but follow the tracks as they was lay down. Peer out the window if ye wish. See for yerself where they go."

McGinley leans out the side window of the engine cab (there is no way to see straight ahead as the boiler sits in front blocking the view). He cranes his neck and now he can just make out in the blackness the gleam of starlight on the rails. Rails that turn and twist impossibly like some deranged design for a rollercoaster, guaranteed to cause riders to shriek and perhaps to vomit.

They are negotiating a pretzel-like turn which is causing some discomfort to McGinley's equilibrium, not to mention his stomach. Suddenly to end the darkness, an encompassing light flairs up with fire and brimstone but curiously, without the heat one would expect from a conflagration of the magnitude of Dante's Inferno. Had they entered the corona of a star? Had a supernova swallowed them? It is a retina-burning blaze that numbs the senses but again, curiously, no damage is done beyond an imaginary one. McGinley staggers.

Then, as soon as it began, it subsides. The train screeches to a halt. McGinley's eyes still see only a glaring hot white like the inside of a lightning bolt, but this soon starts to dissolve. Gradually normal vision returns and McGinley looks out the window. The landscape he sees would be ordinary save for the intensity of its colors. The sky is not just blue, it is vibrant and deep, with cumulus clouds that climb like mountain ranges of crystal. A plain of rolling hills of translucent emerald is flecked with dots of crimson, tangerine, chrome yellow, purest purple—wild flowers of exotic shapes in abundance. There is a river that reflects golden sunlight cutting across the plain, a brilliant gash of fire like a wound on this planet's bosom. And, to McGinley's amazement and delight, there is a station.

The train has stopped at a long, low, red brick building with a red clay tile roof. The roof overhangs a dark brown cobblestone platform. On the platform is a green wooden cart with large, red-painted wheels piled high with trunks and shipping crates and suitcases. A man in a conductor's uniform leans against this, smoking a pipe, the bill of his hat pulled down over his eyes. A gray dog lies at his feet and looks up as the train lets out a blast of steam, the engine's sigh of relief.

The time travelers climb from the train, anxious to be on terra firma once again. The conductor knocks the ashes from his pipe into the palm of his hand and throws them onto the platform. He stands now, waiting for the train's debarking passengers to approach. This they do, having questions and needing answers as never before.

"What is this station?" asks McGinley.

"Why, it is the end of the line, of course," answers the conductor.

"What town is this? What country?" asks Natsumi.

"Better you should ask what planet," replies the conductor with a smirk. He begins to refill his pipe from a pouch of tobacco he takes from his jacket pocket.

"Commandant," Moray yells at the conductor, "Ça ne fait rien! Nous exigeons que le transport. N'y a-t-il pas de chevaux ou de mules?"

The conductor, confused by this onslaught of French which he does not understand coming from a strangely dressed old man, looks to the others for help.

"He wants you to give us that cart and furthermore, conjure up some horses to pull it," says Mary.

"Humph!" says the conductor. "Taxi service is available at the rear of the depot. Have your transfers ready." And with this abrupt dismissal delivered with obvious disdain, he calls for the dog to follow and disappears into the building.

On the other side of the depot a vehicle stands, steam rising from its two rear-mounted boilers. It has four spoked wheels, the two in the rear larger than the two in front in the manner of horse-drawn carriages of nineteenth century Earth (this may not be that same planet, although similarities are suspicious). The sides of the vehicle are decorative with a textured pressed-tin surface in bright green and a shining copper medallion on which is painted the name, "L'Obéissante." The passenger area, large enough for perhaps one-half dozen, is bordered by a railing of turned spindles stained dark red with yellow accents. There is a thin coved roof supported by posts where green velvet curtains are tied back to provide a view in good weather. A mustached man wearing a high top hat sits at the front, his hands resting on a vertically mounted steering wheel.

The driver sees the time travelers approaching and waves to them. "Bonjour, mesa amis. Bienvenue dans ma voiture à vapeur!"

"He says it is a steam carriage," Mary says. "I guess this is the taxi service."

They climb onto the carriage by a short ladder mounted in front to the left of the driver's seat. Mary and the Templar sit just behind the driver and engage him in conversation. Natsumi and McGinley sit in back. The engines boil loudly as the driver gets up a head of steam. Shortly, the carriage starts to move. Gears clatter and the thing sways as it rolls along uneven ground.

A little later, Mary turns toward Natsumi and McGinley and relates what she has learned: "His name is Amédée-Ernest Bollée and they call him Amédée père. He is the inventor of this contraption and recently took it from Paris to Le Mans on a road test where he claims he obtained speeds of over 30 kilometers per hour! That is hard to believe, but he maintains it is true. He was, this morning, in Le Mans and ventured out on the Paris road but drove into a heavy mist and became lost. He does not recognize the countryside here and asks where we are. What should I tell him?"

"Don't tell him anything. Remember how incredulous you were?" says McGinley.

"And still am."

"Where is he driving us, do you know?"

"Moray told him to drive toward the mountains off there in the distance. He thinks there might be a Templar castle up there. Apparently, they were all over the place back in his day."

"Ah, so you admit the Templar is from another time."

"Maybe yes, maybe no. I still may only be dreaming."

"If so, would you please wake up?"

The ridge of blue peaks is not as distant as a seems. They have followed a riverbank lined with peach trees; the pale pink hues of the fruit contrast with the emerald leaves fluttering against a deep cerulean sky. They have discovered a road on the flat plain, rough dirt trampled by hooves and scored by wheel ruts. Someone has come this way; it is a comforting thought…perhaps. They reach the foothills of the mountain in mere hours, a fact which Amédée père attributes to the efficiency of the mechanical design of L'Obéissante. Now to follow the road up the mountain, perhaps to find…

The Old General

Though his quick dart never missed the right eye of a bird,
Now knotted veins and tendons make his left arm like an osier.
He is sometimes at the roadside selling melons from his garden,
He is sometimes planting willows round his hermitage.

In the Three River Provinces, the governors call young men—
And five imperial edicts have summoned the old general.
So he dusts his iron coat and shines it like snow—
Waves his dagger from its jade hilt in a dance of starry steel.

—from "A Song of an Old General" by Wang Wêi (699-759), translated by Witter Bynner from the texts of Kiang Kang-hu.

Wei Shan closes the door of the cage in which he keeps his pet parrot, Bao. The bird, bought from a trader who had journeyed the silk road for many years, is one of Wei Shan's few luxuries. A retired general, even one of his status and renown, is not among the wealthy class. He has but one silk robe which he wears for official visits to Emperor Wu's court when summoned. Such visits have been few these past five years, but now, an emissary has visited Wei Shan in his retreat in the mountains. There is trouble brewing along the border with the Xionqnu nomads. He is needed.

The old general narrows his eyes as he contemplates the turmoil to follow. The Emperor has great generals under his command; Wei Qing and Huo Qubing are certainly capable of strategic planning. He has swordsmen expert with the jian and the dao, the long lance called the pi, and the swordstaff called the sha. He has a calvary force that can handle the lighter crossbows with great effect; the heavier jing nu can hurl sharp javelins and is mounted on chariots.

From a chest of lacquered Zitan wood he takes his helmet of hardened leather, its lightness preferred over the iron equivalent worn by some soldiers. He stands near the window, holding the helmet in front of him as if it is an offering to some benevolent god or goddess. A ray of sunlight strikes it—confirmation from the god or goddess of its suitability for the trials to come. He places it on his head, the familiar feel of it brings confidence and maybe a little anticipation. But then he scowls. Who will water his lilies and prune his chestnut trees?

He hears a noise. Something terrible is coming up the path, snorting and bellowing like the worst monster of nightmares or ghost stories. He goes to the door and looks out. A war chariot the likes of which he has never seen…and he has seen many engines of battle in his time…is coming toward him. This sits high on large wheels and smoke issues from it as if it rides on waves of flame in a sea of brimstone. Strangely, the barbarians within the war wagon are not brandishing weapons, no halberds or dagger axes, no shields, and they wear no armor. What is stranger still is the fact of two women in the chariot!

Wei Shan hails the war chariot. "Nǐ hǎo! Nǐ shì dírén háishì dírén?" (Hello! Are you friend or foe?) He awaits an answer.

Mary Wollstonecraft turns to Natsumi Ito. "What did he say?" she asks.

"He is speaking Mandarin or something close to it. He is Chinese…can't you see that? I am Japanese. I don't speak Mandarin."

"Oh…sorry."

"Judging from his clothing," says McGinley, "he isn't modern. Assuming this is Earth, we must be quite well away into the past...all of our pasts!

Wei Shan does not recognize the dialect he is hearing, much less the language. These barbarians are not Xionqnu. They must be from some faraway land. Has the Emperor sent them to take him to the battle? Has an invasion started? Or are they hostile, even though they have no weapons? What was it that Sun Tzu said? "Victorious warriors win first and then go to war, while defeated warriors go to war first and then seek to win." But he also said, "Quickness is the essence of the war," and "The quality of decision is like the well-timed swoop of a falcon which enables it to strike and destroy its victim."

In such a situation as this, the Old General can swoop—or he can seek to conquer without striking the first blow. He retreats into his house but returns swiftly, his jian in a sheath hung on his side. If they are here to bring him to the battle front, then they will see that he is prepared. If they are here to confront him, perhaps to overpower him by sheer numbers, then they will see that he is able to defend himself. If he senses aggression, he will swoop and swoop with determination and accuracy.

Jacques de Moray, Grand Master of the Knights Templar, climbs down from L'Obéissante and approaches the Old General. He holds his hand out in front of him in the universal gesture of peace. Wei Shan does not feel threatened, but he is cautious. One can use an enemy's own energy against him if one knows how. Wei Shan, having studied both shŏubó and juélì wrestling forms as a youth in his village near the Song Mountains, and being familiar with the writings of Lao Tzu, understands how a "soft" response may overcome a "hard" attack. As a last resort he has his jian. His hand moves automatically toward the hilt of the straight sword but stops short and instead he fingers the red tassel that hangs from it.

Moray gestures toward the sword. May he examine it, he asks in French. Wei Shan gets the gist of the request and again, caution forces him to hesitate. What was it that Confucius said? "Never give a sword to a man who can't dance." And this strange barbarian, although old, looks agile enough to dance quite well. But here are two old soldiers in a grove of willows who have spent a lifetime in war and conflict and have no reason to mistrust each other.

Wei Shan unsheathes the jian and hands it pommel first to the Templar. Moray takes it, tests its heft and balance, and smiles. The Templar is used to the weight and length of his broadsword, the weapon he regrets not having carried at the time of his...abduction? This slender wand of a sword is razor sharp and stiff as the branch of an oak. As he waves the jian in an arc it sings! A wonderful weapon! More substantial than those pig stickers the King's men carry! He hands it back to the old general and compliments him on it, in French. Wei Shan thanks him, in Chinese. They have reached an understanding, not of language, but of attitude.

They have been invited, by so many gestures, to have food with the General. Wei Shan prepares tea in a ceremony that dates back many centuries, warming the pot with hot water before brewing. Bowls of rice are set before the time travelers. Once they are settled and partaking of the food and tea, Wei Shan addresses Natsumi. She is surprised that he speaks to her in Japanese although it is an ancient (for her) dialect and is spoken with a Chinese accent.

He explains: "I was married at a young age to a girl from Wa, the Island of Dwarves, as we call your homeland. Her name was Iyo and she was the daughter of a trader who had come to China bringing with him his wife, two sons, and Iyo. At that time, I was assigned by the head man of our village to trade metal agricultural implements, which the Wa people had in short supply, for the Yayoi pottery from Asahi which Iyo's father had brought. I traveled therefore to the port city of Jimo in the Shandong province, stopping briefly at Lu, which was the home of the sage Confucius.

"By the time I reached Jimo, Iyo's father had been attacked by bandits and he and his sons had been killed. The daughter, not deemed valuable by the bandits because of her heritage, had been abandoned along the road which entered the town from the north, and which I traveled upon in order to reach the port. I found her shivering and hungry and knew I must give aid to her or she too would die.

"At first she was frightened of me, having witnessed my countrymen massacring her family. But I soon gained her confidence and took her with me to Jimo while I performed my duty obtaining pottery for my village. I could not leave her there when it was time to return home so I gave her the option of joining my household, not as a servant, but as a friend and companion. As I could only explain this plan to her using sign language, I was not certain she understood, but apparently, the kindness of my attitude reassured her and she came with me willingly. We grew to admire each other, and it was not long before she joined with me in marriage.

"We taught each other our native languages which was not difficult as Iyo had much learning and could write the Wa characters that are so similar to our own. As you may know, our first Emperor, Qin Shi Huang, searched throughout Wa for immortality potions nearly 200 years ago and trained many of the Wa scholars in the correct forming of the characters of writing. Iyo had studied this kind of writing under the tutelage of an aunt who had lived in the Yamato household as a governess, but that is another story."

"What happened to her?" Natsumi asks after a pause during which she had outlined the General's story to Mary and McGinley, and Mary had relayed it to Moray and Amédée père.

Wei Shan stares for a time at Bao, the parrot. Bao is attacking a large berry, its purple juices drip from her short black curved beak. She has only a vague memory of her life in the dense green rain forest of Arunachal Pradesh in India where she was born and lived before being captured by a Chinese trader. Life in a cage offers no challenges which is good, but no freedom which is bad. Still, she likes her human, as much as a bird can have affection for a man. Her plumage is the green of the forest, her breast a subtle lavender. Greenish-yellow and pale blue tip her tail feathers. She is not brilliantly colored like the parrots of the tropics, but her master thinks she is beautiful.

As he gazes at the parrot, Wei Shan's eyes blur; he is sunk in reverie. What happened to her? Did someone ask that question? What, indeed. Wei Shan was married to Iyo, but young enough to enter military service. And he was called up. In the old days, families could obtain exemption for three boys of age for each horse they donated to the Emperor's war effort. Not so with this Emperor. Emperor Wu had enormous herds—nearly half a million steeds. No need to exempt anyone. Wei Shan left his wife one day when rain pelted down like hammers against brittle steel. His long career in the army of the Han was just beginning. As he remembers that day a tear forms in each eye. Through the tears, he can see her.

She is standing at the clay oven, stirring vegetables in an iron pot. He has entered the room dragging a bag of clothing behind him. This he will take to the training camp. It is now that he tells Iyo. She does not cry nor does she say anything. Her face reveals only a stoicism born of a life of disappointments and tragedies.

"What you must do," he tells her, "is go to my uncle. He will take you in and care for you while I am gone." Still she says nothing. Then he is gone.

He trains with a changzu, a two-bladed lance. His knowledge of shǒubó and juélì wrestling aids him in its mastery. He is now a foot soldier, a hazardous profession, but at least he is surrounded by able archers and his platoon is only backup for the calvary. They are led by a new officer, young Wei Qing who will latter advance to general because of the victory he will achieve in this sneak attack on the Xiongnu at Longcheng. The enemy has eluded the Han for many years now and occupies lands the Han would have for their own. The battle is bloody. The Xiongnu defeat is devastating and forces them to retreat to the Northern Gobi Dessert. Wei Shan now is able to return home.

He has been gone for two years. He goes immediately to the house of his uncle. Anxious to see Iyo once again he knocks on the door. There is no answer. He knocks again, this time more loudly, Still no answer, not a sound from inside the house. He goes to the window and peers inside. The interior is dark. His resolve overcomes his sense of good deportment. He throws open the door and enters his uncle's house. It is empty. There is no furniture, no sign that anyone is living here. No uncle, no Iyo!

Wei Shan hurries along a dirt road that winds through a series of gardens and orchards in order to get to the nearest neighbor's house. The man who lives there has taken produce from his garden to the market but his wife, a woman named Ling, is at home. Where has his uncle disappeared to and where is the woman who he had taken in? Ling only knows that one year ago the uncle, Lei Kun, left for the capital city, having been summoned into service for the government because of his expertise as a scribe. The woman must have gone with him, but she cannot say for sure.

Wei Shan journeys to Chang'an in the northwestern province of Shaanxi. He is three months on rock-strewn roads through mountain passes and along rushing streams. Some call the capital Xijing. It was founded in 195 BCE and it is the eastern most terminus of the Silk Road. The final phase of his journey takes him along the banks of the Wei River. Here he reaches the outer walls of the city. A gate on the northwest side allows him entrance to the Nine Markets area which serves travelers and traders from the Silk Road. Where to find Iyo?

At a market booth selling fresh melons he learns that a man employed as a government scribe would most likely be found at the Weiyang Palace. The palace sits on a high point along a ridge and is surrounded by tall walls. Its rectangular shape affords it four gates, the northmost of which is used by commoners, the others by nobles and foreign emissaries. It is doubtful, his informant tells him, that Wei Shan will be admitted past the main terrace, as the north gate has been closed since the recent occurrence of unrest among the populace over religious changes the Emperor is making. Emperor Wu is an advocate of Confucianism; this is unpopular.

Wei Shan finds the north gate and indeed is prevented from entering by a guard. But fortune smiles upon him as he recognizes the guard as being a man who had attended military training at the very same camp as Wei Shan, a man named Bo Zedong. Fortune, like the elegant jian, is a very sharp double-edged sword, as Wei Shan is about to learn.

Wei Shan introduces himself as a comrade in arms from the not so distant past and luckily the man remembers him. He explains his quest, to find his uncle and ultimately his wife. But the story troubles the guard. The uncle was no doubt housed in the palace where his duties as scribe would necessitate his formal presence. The woman, however, would not be allowed inside the royal court. There was one possibility, Bo Zedong says. She may have been taken as a concubine in which case she would be housed in the harem residence. The harem was off limits to everyone. There was, however, one way to gain access to the residence…a very risky way.

Unknown to most of the populace, the palaces of Chang'an, Weiyang Palace, Changle Palace, Epang Palace and others, are connected by a series of underground tunnels. There are guard stations at intervals along these tunnels. Bo Zedong, typically corrupt, has, for a small fee, given Wei Shan instructions on how to obtain the costume of a palace eunuch. The day following, dressed in this elaborate disguise, Wei Shan is back at the north gate where Bo Zedong waits for him with a crudely drawn map of the tunnels.

"This route," says Bo Zedong, tracing his finger along the maze of lines, "should take you past the fewest guard stations. Just look as if you belong there, and you may not have any problems."

The tunnels are surprisingly well lit and not at all damp and foreboding as Wei Shan had feared. A scruffy rodent follows him for a short time, then disappears into a crack in the wall. The first guard station is not occupied. The second contains two soldiers who look at Wei Shan with disdain, then ignore him; his disguise is working! At a third he is challenged. He acts dumb and points to his ears to indicate deafness. This seems to work as the guard is reluctant to waste his time with a stupid eunuch.

He reaches the harem and stops at the doorway. He is filled with wonder as he views the interior of the chamber. Exotic silks from India are hung on the walls. Intricately patterned cloths cover low divans. Paper lanterns of the brightest red hang from the ceiling. Through an archway on the other side of the chamber he can see a courtyard containing a lush garden and a pool of blue water where water lilies float and golden fish are swimming. Willows dip branches toward the pool like gentle rain in an ink drawing. Women in brilliantly colored silk robes come and go through the chamber and in the courtyard. Their hair is styled with combs of silver and jade. Their feet wear jeweled slippers.

He waits and watches. Is Iyo among these women of dreamlike beauty? He could call out for her, but he is afraid guards may come if he does. One of the harem concubines has noticed him and approaches. Summoning courage, or perhaps throwing away caution, Wei Shan asks her if a woman lives here who came from the island called Wa. The woman is shocked to be quizzed like this by a eunuch. But she senses there is something about this eunuch that is different. He is afraid and desperate and bold enough to ask for her help. Why does he want to find this woman from Wa?

"Her name is Iyo. She was my wife before she came here. I was off to war and returned to find her gone. I must see her again, see that she lives and is well. Will you help me?"

The concubine is touched by Wei Shan's plea and now she understands that he is not a eunuch but a lover. Lovers must be aided…there is not enough true romance here in the harem. "Wait here one moment," she tells him. She disappears through the arch and into the courtyard. Several minutes elapse during which Wei Shan begins to sweat. Will she come back with the guards? No, they are not allowed in the harem residence. But what?

The woman returns with a second woman in tow. Wei Shan does not recognize Iyo at first. She is too exotic, too beautifully made up in the manner of a concubine. There is a tearful reunion and they embrace. The other woman, shocked and now very much afraid of the consequences of this act if it is observed by the senior members of the harem, retreats hurriedly. Wei Shan too realizes their peril. There is only one recourse: to run.

They enter the tunnel hoping to evade the guards. At the first guard station shouts ring out. Footfalls behind them spurs them on to a greater pace. Now they are running, their breath in gasps. At the next guard station the two men are standing in the tunnel to block their passage, swords in hand. Wei Shan, now remembering his martial arts training, stops just short of them, holding his hands out as if in surrender, As one of the guards advances to grab him, Wei Shan uses the man's momentum to pull him forward, he pivots, and throws the man to one side. The other guard now comes at him. This one too is bested. The fugitives continue their flight for freedom.

Impossibly, they have made it all the way to the north gate. Bo Zedong is there and steps aside to let them pass. But, as the guard knows he will be held responsible for their escape, he betrays them by yelling for help. More guards materialize to pursue the fugitives. Wei Shan and Iyo are running now toward the bridge which connects the city and its suburbs. They are almost across the Wei River when the arrows begin to fly. He has her hand in his when she is hit. She falls, bleeding. Wei Shan picks her up and carries her the rest of the way to the other shore. He ducks into a wooded area where a dense stand of brush hides them from the pursuing guards. They are saved from capture. But…

"How sad," says Natsumi. "She died in your arms? The love of your life. And you have lived alone ever since. You returned to the army and rose through the ranks to become a general. And now you have retired to this mountain retreat."

"And now," says the Old General, "They are calling me back."

The Old General has gotten his armor and his jian and a few odds and ends including several day's supply of dried fruits and vegetables and has stood by the door of his small house to say goodbye to his new-found friends. Jacques de Moray has expressed a desire to accompany Wei Shan into battle. "If I return to my own time I will just be captured and probably burned at the stake for heresy," he says. "I would rather fall in battle." Wei Shan rummages through the chest where he stores military items and returns to the Templar carrying a dao. This is a Chinese saber, flat and curved and very very sharp. At first, Moray mistakes it for the type of sword used by the Saracens called a scimitar.

"This is much superior to the scimitar," Moray says. "Not so good for thrusting like your jian, but it will take off a head quite nicely." Natsumi translates.

Amédée père offers the use of L'Obéissante to transport the warriors to the battle front. He is intrigued by the prospect of witnessing an ancient battle, although he does not volunteer to add his name to the ranks of the Han army. Still, another suit of armor is found near the bottom of the old chest and given to the Frenchman. Wei Shan thrusts a light crossbow into his hands. Amédée père just smiles meekly. One of the willow trees now falls to the axe to feed the double steam engines that drive L'Obéissante.

"Can I drop you anywhere?" Amédée asks Mary Wollstonecraft.

"Nineteenth century England would be nice," she answers. "The others might like America in the twentieth century. I guess we we're all out of luck in that respect."

Wei Shan has offered to let the English-speaking time travelers stay in his house until he returns...if he returns. "Just water the melon patch and chase away the rats that come to feast on my vegetable garden," he requests.

L'Obéissante chugs down the dirt road, spitting rings of gray smoke into the air. The others settle in. Mary is somewhat jealous of Natsumi's intimacy (plutonic at this point) with McGinley. She has always been attracted to older men. She misses Shelley but...what is the expression? Never stare a dark horse in the mouth, or something like that. Natsumi feels no sense of camaraderie with the soon-to-be famous English writer. Soon, that is, if ever they get back. McGinley, who is used to sitting still, finds a comfortable chair, and hunkers down to await the sunset. His eyes slowly close and soon he is dreaming; he is in his rocker on his porch in Tennessee and his cat, Scheherazade, is curled on his lap.

Mary and Natsumi explore the Old General's abode. He is not rich, but he has accumulated an assortment of elegant furniture and accoutrements to give the impression of a luxurious existence. Mary thinks such a display of elegance shows the lack of a virtuous life but says nothing. They find an old chest decorated with carvings of dragons and stylized clouds. They open this and inside is a neatly folded robe of green silk, a hanfu, or pao, like those worn by nobles. Natsumi unfolds the kimono. It has wide sleeves and a sash with a jade clasp.

"It is small," says Natsumi, "but I wonder if it would fit me."

"Women," says Mary, "concentrate upon the way they look instead of what is in their minds. Of course, nothing much has been put in their minds in the first place."

"Mary, that is unfair. I just wondered…oh, look! The holes on the back of the kimono. And the stains!"

"Do you think this was the robe worn by Iyo, his wife? Did he keep it all these years? An obsession with the death of a loved one! How fitting for a general. Ugh…war! Percy has said that man has no right to kill his brother, and that to do so in uniform only adds the infamy of servitude to the crime of murder."

"There is an old Japanese proverb," says Natsumi, "that Duty is as heavy as a mountain, but Death is as light as a feather."

And while the two women talk of life and death and the foolishness of men, the steam-driven carriage makes its way toward destiny. All our yesterdays, said Shakespeare, have lighted fools the way to dusty death. But for these fools, the light flickers and begins to fade. Night is falling early, thinks the Old General. But night is an abstract, a concept born of the rotation of planets. And what planet is this?

On the planet called Earth (in Wei Shan's comprehension of reality) it is January of 119 BCE. Emperor Wu has directed General Huo Qubing to proceed with his forces from Dai Prefecture to attack the Xiongnu tribes deep in the Gobi Desert. General Wei Qing is approaching the enemy from Dingxiang simultaneously. The nomads have a well-trained cavalry of over one hundred thousand, but the Han have armored chariots which are arranged in ring formation creating a virtual fortress which is impossible to penetrate. The Han will ultimately be victorious at this, the Battle of Mobei.

But this is not planet Earth. It is a place on the edge of eternity—the intersection of the reality that the Old General perceives and the reality of one hundred billion tomorrows that await the pending whim of fate. The light fades, not for lack of star emitted energy, but because this transition proceeds at a right angle to its tomorrow. L'Obéissante wobbles as it traces a course along the edge. Amédée stills sees, or thinks he sees, the forests and mountains and rivers of that world that resides in his mind's eye, albeit darkened by the premature dusk. If he were to glance downward, then he might see an errant star, a delinquent galaxy, or a dwindling comet.

The blackness becomes total. Then suddenly, there is a flash and L'Obéissante comes to rest on a quiet street in Le Mans, France, in 1873. Amédée-Ernest Bollée turns to address his passengers, but Jacques de Moray and Wei Shan are no longer in the carriage. He brings his hands to his face, covers his eyes for a moment, then removes them and looks around. Across a broad square he can see the Cathédrale Saint Julien-Le Mans. There is only one explanation: he has dozed off and has had the most peculiar dream. Funny, though, he does not remember getting the willow branches he now sees stacked up at the back of the carriage and ready to feed the twin steam engines.

Jacques de Moray is momentarily blinded by the flash of light that punctuates this ride through descending darkness in L'Obéissante. He now finds that he is no longer on the steam carriage but is standing in the courtyard near the Great Hall of the Tour du Temple in the Knights Templar compound just outside of Paris, France. It is October 13, 1307. There is something lurking in his memory that he cannot quite bring into his consciousness. It is something about a young English girl who is warning him of impending doom. C'est ridicule! It is too lovely a day to dwell on melancholy improbabilities. In his hand he holds a sword with a curved blade that broadens near the tip. It resembles a scimitar but it is thinner and more polished. Where in the world did I get this, he thinks.

Wei Shan recovers from the blinding flash to observe that the air around him is filled with a raging sandstorm. He is among the left flank of the Han General Wei Qing's force of infantry men who are about to renew their attack against Chanyu's Xiongnu army. The enemy greatly outnumbers them, but the surprise attack will kill 19,000 and chase the rest deep into the Khangai Mountains where the Han will capture the Zhao Xin Fortress. Wei Shan has had little time to think about the strange visitors he had entertained so recently at his mountain retreat. When he does have time to reminisce, the vision he will evoke will be that of his lost love, Iyo.

The battles are decisive for the Han. The Xiongnu have retreated and the Han have reclaimed the territories they have long desired. Wei Shan begins the long journey home. This will have been his last campaign. The landscape through which he walks is strangely radiant, as if an internal glow emanates from a hidden domain of fire demons. An illusion, the result of hot sand underneath thin shoes. A hot desert wind blows against him, impeding his progress. What is that ahead? A bank of gray mist.

Natsumi has been sharing the bedroom with Mary for these past two weeks while Madison McGinley sleeps in the front room. Natsumi wishes it was Mary Wollstonecraft sleeping in the front room but McGinley is too much of a gentleman to engage in an affair that would inconvenience the third person of their party. Not that Mary would be shocked. Perhaps another reason causes his reluctance. My God, Natsumi thinks…here we are trapped in another world, another universe…no noisy neighbors, no decorum to maintain. No one present would be shocked, accept, perhaps, McGinley himself! Natsumi is unhappy.

For one thing, Mary Wollstonecraft snores. For another, she often wakes in the middle of the night calling out as some nightmare torments her. Mary has told Natsumi she will not account to anyone for the dreams: they are her own and a refuge and a pleasure no matter how annoying. She could write them down, she says, and the specter that haunts her midnight pillow would terrify and fascinate whoever dared read them. Natsumi has not told Mary Wollstonecraft what she knows about the future Mary Shelley and the miserable monster she will create. Or maybe never will get to create if things go on as they have.

At breakfast Mary relates the dream that woke her in the night to Natsumi and McGinley. Partaking of freshly picked fruits from the garden and tea brewed from the Old General's store of black leaf, they listen attentively. It concerns a man, an alchemist of the type of Cornelius Agrippa or Albertus Magnus, she tells them. This reference to alchemy greatly interests McGinley, having traveled extensively (through time and space) with the alchemist, Lorcan Mac Conmara. At this juncture he does not mention this fact to Mary.

The alchemist in the dream, Mary says, through intensive study of human anatomy and experimenting with alchemy, has discovered the cause of the generation of life. He believes he is capable of bestowing animation upon nonliving matter. In the dream he takes Mary on a tour of his workshop. There she witnesses a morbid collection of bones and tissue samples from dissecting rooms and other unfathomable sources. On a shelf is a row of human and animal skulls, their empty eye sockets stare at her accusingly. In the open mouth of one of the skulls is a large black beetle. With a hiss, the insect jumps at her, waking her up.

"Yes," says Natsumi, "I remember that moment. The moonlight illuminated our bedroom and when you woke with a rather lengthy ululation, I could see you were dripping with sweat."

"It was a warm night. The dream did unnerve me somewhat, but I assure you these nocturnal fantasies are great entertainment for me. They do not represent anything about the nature of my persona nor of my soul."

"I don't believe I said anything about your soul," quips Natsumi. "Perhaps you should write your dreams down. There are people that like to read such chilling tales."

"Natsumi," cautions McGinley, "Mary will take pen in hand of her own accord, should she wish to do so. Your suggestion is unnecessary."

"Just trying to be helpful."

"My poet friends and I often tell each other ghost stories on stormy nights. Percy says that the great instrument of moral good is imagination. The macabre and the melancholy are as important as stimulants as the idyllic and the arcadian."

The next night it is Natsumi who has the nightmare. Back in 1931 she had seen the James Whale film of *Frankenstein* starring Boris Karloff as the monster. Like many theater goers of the time it had frightened her out of her wits. Now the monster from the film comes to her in a dream. It is the scene from the film where Karloff's monster has just thrown a young girl into a lake where she is drowned. Natsumi watches this horrific scene from off camera, but the monster senses her presence and comes at her. She runs and Karloff/monster races after her, plodding along with his ungainly frame and growling as only Karloff can. She trips and falls. He is on her, drags her to the lake and hurls her into it. Natsumi has been struggling all through this to wake up but cannot seem to regain consciousness. There is something in the water that grabs and shakes her. It is Mary Wollstonecraft and now she awakes.

"Why dear, you're sweating," says Mary.

If Mary never gets back to Switzerland to write her novel, thinks Natsumi, then the film will never be made, and I won't have that nightmare. She realizes that this is a guilty thought, but it appeals to her need for revenge against this snippy young girl. Then she understands the paradox: because she did have the dream, Mary Wollstonecraft will certainly return to her own time and write her novel at the retreat in Switzerland. This gives her hope.

But weeks drag on. The Old General has still not returned from the war. The space-time vortex has not reappeared. The horrific dreams no longer come, but that is little compensation. They wonder...what now? It is a pleasant prison in which to do time, however. The willows sway elegantly in the gentle wind. Blue birds alight in the garden, feasting on insects. McGinley has devised a clever rat trap to rid the gardens of the many vermin and so the melon harvest is plentiful. The time travelers take the melons in a pushcart to the market in the valley and trade for necessities. Some of the locals they meet wonder about this European man living up on the mountain with his two wives. The language barrier remains so that no socializing is possible. No one thinks to visit them.

Autumn is beginning to turn the willow leaves to gold and the sparse grass to umber. There is a nip in the air. Mary is out for a walk on one of the many mountain paths that crisscross their realm. A few late wildflowers line the path. The tree line can be seen at a higher altitude where wisps of cloud hurry across the azure sky. An unfamiliar path diverges from her normal route—she has not noticed this one before. She follows it, serpentine and beckoning and mysterious though it is. A chance to allay the boredom of this time of waiting.

She rounds an outcropping of shale and comes upon a flat plateau which lies in shade so deep that it is moments before her eyes adjust. But then she sees the thing that sits there. It is black and nearly invisible in the gloom. It is clearly not natural for it has a shape like an enormous globe and there seems to be a slight hum emanating from it. Mary hurries back to the house to tell the others.

She leads Natsumi and McGinley to the plateau. The thing is still there. McGinley knows what it is and that impossibly, it is the time machine which stands there before them and which had been invented so many lifetimes ago by an evil scientist. How can this be? The darkness veils the fact of its semi-translucence. Slowly, McGinley becomes aware of this phenomenon. The time machine is only partly in their space-time. Now he notices another object: a mortar shell which hangs from the surface of the sphere as if it is frozen in time just as it is about to strike. It is about to explode, but its real time is in lockstep with the machine and the machine is traveling along a space-time vector—the machine is in between the there from which it came and the here of now. If the time machine fully materializes…

Fugit Inreparabile Tempus

When the time machine was standing in the parking lot of the Roundhouse Memorial Park in Raton, New Mexico, automatic weapons were being fired at it by John Dillinger's men. Riordan, seeing the assault through the transparent wall of the sphere (transparent from the inside out but not from the outside in) yelled a warning to Mac Conmara and the alchemist began fiddling with the buttons and dials and levers on the control panel,

Bullets bounced harmlessly to the ground from the surface of the time machine. Dillinger's bodyguards then brought forth an army surplus bazooka, dropped in a very lethal shell, and fired the weapon point blank at the time machine. The shell struck the time machine just at the instant that Mac Conmara activated the transformation sequence. The sphere leaped through space-time carrying the shell, still unexploded, along with it.

The place where Dr. Madison McGinley, Natsumi Ito, and Mary Wollstonecraft were standing, a shady plateau in the mountains of a planet that was not the Earth of the Han Dynasty of China (but overlapped its space-time sufficiently to contain people and events from that era), was coming and going into view through the wall of the time machine. A visual vibration. The sensation, for Riordan Ó Ciardha, Lorcan Mac Conmara, and Ríona Ó Brádaigh was the visual equivalent of sticking one's finger in an electric light socket. Mac Conmara had intended to return to Ríona's planet in the alternate universe on the other side of the Big Bang, but obviously something had gone wrong. They were stuck on the edge of the time vortex and this might not even be Ríona's planet.

"Master," the alchemist's apprentice said to him, "I have two observations to report. First, there are three people outside that I can just barely make out as we are sort of wavering on the brink of materializing. One of them closely resembles Dr. McGinley. Second, there is an unexploded shell touching the outside surface of the time machine. Of course, it is hard to be certain, but I would suggest that it will explode once we do materialize."

Mac Conmara considered this. If he were more familiar with the workings of the time machine, he might find a way of slipping away from the shell before it exploded. But he was not. Could they open the door and jump out? Set the machine for another space-time leap with just enough delay to make it out the door? It was worth a try. The exploding shell might not destroy the time machine completely, but it certainly would kill McGinley and his companions.

"Riordan, Ríona, I want you to be ready to exit the time machine when I give you the signal. I'm setting the machine for a slightly delayed space-time leap. I'm hoping we will land on firm ground and not in some void between realities."

The vibration, a wavering as Riordan described it, was slowing. They seemed to enter the new space-time for as long as a few seconds before fading again into an oblivion of endless darkness. Mac Conmara set the coordinates to return to New Mexico at the exact time they had left. He waited for the new reality they had observed to appear and then shouted, "Now!" The three time travelers jumped out of the door and fell to the ground in front of McGinley and company. The sphere vibrated one last time and, silhouetted against a flash of light, it disappeared.

It materialized in the parking lot of the Roundhouse Memorial Park in Raton, New Mexico. The exploding shell knocked the time machine at an acute angle to the reality of that space-time and sent it into the unknown. The shell, energized by the time vortex, erupted with such a fury that Sheriff Horace Kilby, Officer Robert "Bud" Brooks, Officer Pete Peterson, Mayor James Lawrence who was actually John Dillinger, and Dillinger's two bodyguards, the assault force that had been riddling the time machine with bullets and the mortar shell, were killed instantly by the blast.

"Mac Conmara," said McGinley, helping the alchemist to his feet, "is it really you?"

"Who were you expecting?" Mac Conmara asked.

"I was hoping it was not Nikolai Borisov, the so-called mad scientist who invented that thing."

"We left him on a planet in another universe…dead, I'm afraid. It's a long story."

Introductions were in order. Riordan translated into Gaelic for Ríona, who was only just starting to learn English. Names, eras, and backgrounds exchanged, the six, an oddly matched assortment of immigrants to the edge of eternity, began to make their way back to the Old General's mountain retreat. As they rounded the outcropping of shale which had cast a heavy shade onto the plateau, it was Riordan who first spoke:

"I thought you said this was China in the Han Dynasty, around 100 BC. If so, why are we staring down the side of this mountain at a bunch of skyscrapers?"

"That wasn't there before," exclaimed Mary Wollstonecraft.

But there is was: a shining city nestled in a quiet valley. There was something familiar in the configuration of those tall buildings. Two rose together as twins near the edge of a large river that ran along one side of the metropolis. There was a second river on the city's other side and they came to meet at the apex of the city, as if that great habitat sat on an island. Then they saw a vast green area near the middle of…

"Oh my God, it's New York City!" said McGinley.

They stared at the city that was called The Big Apple for a time. McGinley and Natsumi recognized NYC but the cluster of giant skyscrapers was unfamiliar. This must be a New York of the future…all of their futures. The twin towers of the World Trade Center (they did not know the name of this complex) dwarfed other more familiar landmarks like the Empire State Building and the Chrysler Building. They could see cars and people swarming through the canyon-like streets. The old cliché about people looking like ants came to mind.

Riordon broke the silence: "Can we get down there?" he asked.

"The slope here is pretty steep. We better look for a path with some switchbacks if that is indeed what we plan to do," answered McGinley.

"If a metropolis has mysteriously appeared in the valley, New York or not, then does that mean that the Old General's house is no longer where it was?" asked Mary.

"Sounds like you are finally getting the drift of how this space-time shifting works," said McGinley.

"I'm afraid so."

"Doctor," said Riordon, "our time machine has flown off back in time…or maybe ahead in time…to New Mexico, and probably exploded. At any rate, we are marooned here. There is a nice big city down there and it is probably full of humans. I vote we go down there."

"What, no dinosaurs?" said Mary. "How disappointing."

Ríona touched Riordan's shoulder. "I'm never going to get home, am I?" she whispered to him.

"We'll see, my love. At least we are together. This new world can't be all bad. Look at the size of those buildings! It must be a vigorous world full of happy people that know how to build things and live prosperous and secure lives."

But (the edge of eternity was replete with buts—it was chock full of them) security was about to become a non sequitur. As they gazed down at New York, New York, an airliner, American Airlines Flight 111, hijacked by Islamic terrorists, crashed into the North Tower of the World Trade Center between the 93rd and 99th floors. As the airplane hit the building, a huge fireball erupted. The tower, the highest in the world when it was first completed, stood 1,362 feet high; flames licked up to the roof trapping people on the floors above. Burning debris began to fall, igniting the buildings and other structures below. The time travelers, high on the mountain, where frozen with disbelief and terror at the sight.

"We must certainly be in some alternate universe," said McGinley. "This sort of thing could never happen in our America."

"It is catastrophic indeed," said Mac Conmara. "But like the old Irish saying, there's no need to fear the wind if your haystacks are tied down."

"That makes no sense," said Mary. "It's bloody stupid!"

"I mean that if you are raising buildings so high into the firmament, some kind of bird is going to fly into them. A metal one, at that!"

"Madison," said Natsumi, "I'm frightened. It makes me think of Nagaski. Do you suppose…?"

"Just an awful accident. No one in their right mind would…"

And just then, United Airlines Flight 175, also hijacked by Islamic terrorists, crashed into the South Tower between the 77th and 85th floors. Both airliners had been full of aviation fuel. The heat and the flames were intense. Nearly everyone in the floors above the impact areas was killed. 14 people managed to escape down a stairway in the South tower. Some of those trapped jumped from windows. Beneath the impact areas pandemonium reigned. Fire engines began racing through the streets toward the World Trade Center.

"You still want to go down there, young man?" McGinley asked Riordan.

"I guess not," he answered.

"Can we go back and see if maybe the Old General's place is still there?" asked Natsumi.

"I remember which path it was," said Mary. "Follow me."

They had been walking for an hour but there was no sign of the house or of the gardens or any familiar landscape. The path was slowly descending the mountain. They still had a view of the city below and the billows of smoke issuing from the twin towers. They paused for a moment to look at the destruction when the South Tower collapsed. An upper section of the tower had fallen onto the floor below and had initiated a structural collapse like a toppling roll of dominoes. Floor by floor the supporting columns failed. Concrete from the crushed floors reached the ground level and then the sequence of column failures moved upward. Walls peeled from the building and fell on adjacent structures. The South Tower seemed to be shrinking down into the ground, swallowed into an expanding cloud of dust.

"Oh my God!" rose the collective lament. "Nagasaki, Hiroshima," said Natsumi.

One half hour later, the North Tower collapsed. Fires were raging among other buildings in the World Trade Center complex. A dust cloud reached three miles from the epicenter. Nearly 3,000 people died in or around the World Trade Center including over 400 fire fighters and other emergency personnel. On the world of Earth, on September 11, 2001, another two airliners were hijacked. One, American Airlines Flight 77, struck the Pentagon and the other, United Airlines Flight 93, crashed in a field in Pennsylvania before reaching its target which might have been the White House. On this world, the one at the edge of eternity, it was impossible to know about these other occurrences. In fact…

"Look!" said Riordan, pointing down at this New York City which lay impossibly in a valley on an alternate world in an alternate universe. New York City began to flicker and fade like the image from a film projector which had a faulty bulb. In an instant, NYC was gone, and in its place lay a peaceful valley with trees and meadows and streams—a storybook vista with no evidence of the 911 catastrophe.

"I'm still having trouble believing all this," said Mary.

"And you're the one with the vivid imagination," said Natsumi.

Loose pebbles stared rolling down from the slope above them, spilling onto the path like a storm of hail balls. The staccato of particles drowned out any conversation about who had imagination and who did not. Some of the pebbles were light blue, some pale green. Turquoise? Jade? The size of the particles increased. It seemed a good time to get off the path, but to one side was the steep slope down to the valley and on the other was the cascade of rocks. They ran. The path was narrow here and the party negotiated it single file: Indian style, as McGinley remembered it being called from his long past childhood. Racial insensitivity, he now thought. Funny the things you think about during times of stress!

The path curved, steepened, then ran under an overhang. This gave them a momentary reprieve from the avalanche, but the rocks now were small boulders. They could not go forward nor backward on the path. They moved further back under the overhang as the deluge of boulders began to rotate, as if blown in the swirling wind of a cyclone. The scene before them grew darker as the number of boulders increased. They inched further back. Some of the boulders began to settle on the path. Slowly a wall of stone formed, blocking the entrance. They were being trapped inside a dark cave!

Ríona hugged Riordan tightly. "I'm afraid," she said.

Natsumi found McGinley's hand and clutched it; he did not move away but tried to survey their stone prison with what little light remained. He could see that the chamber extended back even further than where they had retreated and now stood. Perhaps…

Mac Conmara also examined the chamber and started toward the back of it finding that it turned, and that a tunnel was just behind the turn. "If only we had a torch," he said.

"Will this do?" asked Mary, taking a small box of Lucifers from a reticle that hung from her shoulder. She struck one of the matches against the stone and the flare illuminated the odd turning. "Shall I lead the way?" she then asked, and without waiting for an answer, entered the tunnel. "Ouch!" she exclaimed as the match burned down to her fingertips. She lit another and held it high so the others could follow.

The tunnel had a slight downward slope but the walls and ceiling afforded a wide pathway. "Indian style" single file was not necessary so the time travelers proceeded two by two. Mary and Mac Conmara were in the lead. Mary had so far struck six matches and now only two remained. The end of the tunnel was not in view. Suddenly, Mac Conmara stumbled on something that lay on the tunnel floor. Something round and brittle, which shattered underfoot. Leaning with match in hand to examine the object, Mary let out a gasp, and then began to giggle.

"What in the world?" McGinley asked.

The thing stared up at Mary with empty sockets. "It's just a skull," she said. "A very old one, I would guess." The match burned out and she lit the second to the last.

As the flare of the igniting Lucifer lit up the tunnel, Riordan made a discovery. On the wall, in an old iron bracket, was an unlit torch: a wooden stick wrapped in linen that had been soaked in paraffin, judging by the smell of it. He retrieved it and held it to Mary's burning match. It burst into a nice bright flame and details of the tunnel came into view.

The floor was made of cobblestone and the walls were stone hewed flat by some sort of tool. The tunnel twisted to the left here and around the corner was a wooden door. Above the door was a sign lettered in an antique script. It read: "Arrête, c'est ici l'empire de la mort!"

"What's that say?" asked Riordan.

Mary answered: "Stop! This is the empire of death!"

"Well, I'm game if you are," replied Riordan. "Ladies first?"

"Absolutely!"

They swung the door open. It moved with a creak and a groan, as if it were echoing the warning of the sign above it. Into the empire of death went Mary and Riordan, followed by the others. Along the walls were niches in which were stacked bones—not helter-skelter, but in arrangements that appeared to have been artistically designed. Skulls were stacked in pyramids, femurs stood upright as if supporting invisible bodies. As they moved along the tunnel they saw hundreds, thousands of such displays. Here and there were broken headstones and statuary which might have graced a cemetery above ground but which had fallen into decline and come to be stored along with the remains of the dead.

"You know where we are," Mary said, not phrasing this as a question. "This is the catacombs of Paris. Old mining tunnels that were appropriated as early as the 1700s to relocate bodies from other cemeteries to a suitable ossuary. There was a foul-smelling cemetery called the Saint's Innocents where a wall collapsed, exposing all the decaying corpses. First they dumped them into an old well but later moved them to the mining tunnels. A man named Louis-Étienne Héricart de Thury did the arranging. An artist, was he not?"

Natsumi was not surprised that Mary Wollstonecraft knew so much about the catacombs of Paris, given her interest in death and resurrection. It did not look as if there would be any resurrection in this place, however. Just as well. But was this Paris? They ventured through the wide tunnels of the catacombs with its wall of skulls. Inset into one wall was a stone plaque in the shape of a cross. On this were inscribed the words, "Ossemens de L'Englise et du Cloître des Capucins S. Honoré le 20 Mars 1804." Bones from the Capuchin Convent of Saint-Honoré, founded in 1576 by Catherine de Médicis, seized during the French Revolution, and razed in 1804. Yes, this must be Paris.

André Lemaire grumbled to himself (there was no one around to complain to) as he pushed the hand cart down the rue d'Enfer past the toll gathering buildings of the Barrière d'Enfer on his way to the catacombs of Paris. Beneath a cloth covering in the cart were six partially decomposed bodies from the graveyard at Notre-Dame-des-Blancs-Manteaux. Inspector Héricart de Thury would not be pleased if André tarried along the way and yet he was compelled to stop and gaze up at the friezes on the neo-classical pavilions of the Barrière d'Enfer which depicted, in stone relief, dancing maidens.

The entrance to the catacombs was at the east building, the headquarters of the Inspector General. The ossuary was now open to the public and André had heard that Francis I, the Austrian Emperor, was to tour here in the following weeks. Mon Deu! The conquering demon wanted a look-see. Besides the artistic array of bones and artifacts from the old cemeteries there were special rooms for the display of minerals found at Paris and its surrounds, as well as a sort of museum for oddities and skeletal deformities. Ladies of the court seemed particularly interested in the oddities.

When he reached the entrance to the catacombs he found Inspector Héricart de Thury waiting there. The Inspector scrutinized André with a frown. "What is this?" he asked André.

"The last of the poor souls from Le Marais," André answered.

"You are supposed to move the bodies at night so as not to alarm the neighbors."

"I ventured out quite late last night and only now have arrived. My duty was delayed, not by my own negligence, but because of the return of the King."

André Lemaire was referring to King Louis XVIII who had just reentered Paris after the so-called Hundred Days of Napoleon Bonaparte's own return from exile, the invasion of Paris by coalition armies of Prussian and England, and the subsequent abdication of the Emperor. Passionate and raucous days, indeed.

"The crowds…"

"None of your concern. The design of the chamber for Notre-Dame-des-Blancs-Manteaux must be completed before Friday. Get these bones into the tunnel at once!"

"Yes, Monsieur. Immediately."

Access for catacomb visitors at the Barrière d'Enfer was via a spiral staircase so André pushed the cart down the Avenue du parc Montsouris where there was a maintenance well he could lower his cart into using a block and tackle. Now he went into the tunnel, stopping to light a torch. It was some distance to the main ossuary through this part of the old quarry. Several passages led off in different directions, but he knew the way to the site where he was to deliver the bodies.

Yes, he knew the layout of the tunnels here below the streets of Paris, the old, abandoned quarries and the excavations that once had collapsed swallowing houses and stores into the underworld. Most were closed off now, filled in with mud or debris, or, like the catacombs, repurposed to rid Paris of its stinking, above-ground cemeteries and its trash heaps. There were over 300 kilometers of hallways and galleries and the necropolis housed over six million corpses. Knowledgeable about the maze of the underground of Paris, still he kept to the usual route. Even he could get lost.

There was a story he had heard about the man named Philibert Aspairt. Aspairt had been the Val-de-Grâce Hospital's doorkeeper. In 1793 he had entered the catacombs looking for the rumored treasure of the Carthusian Monks supposedly hidden there. He became lost and died. His body was found 11 years later in the tunnel under the rue l'Enfer. In 1804 Inspector Héricart de Thury built a monument to the lost man on the spot where his body was found. The Inspector had built or maintained many monuments and curiosities of the mining tunnels: the Chartreux Fountain, the Cubes Room with its large cubic blocks, The Mansart Stairway beneath the Val de Grâce, the Crypt with its stone carving of a delicate rose by Gandalf and La Gargouille, the Montsouris Gallery where a damp and dark petrifying spring had been nicknamed the Jellyfish. André Lemaire had seen it all; he didn't need to see it again.

Mary Wollstonecraft was musing to herself as she strolled listlessly through the hallways of death. So deliciously melancholy. The torch cast shadows, lengthening skull shapes…did the spirits of the dead flit about, livid with the hue of death and decay? Some lines from Coleridge's "Ancient Mariner" came to mind. When the mariner sees the crew die:

The souls did from their bodies fly,—
They fled to bliss or woe!
And every soul, it passed me by,
Like the whizz of my CROSS-BO

And when he sees them rise:

They groaned, they stirred, they all uprose,
Nor spake, nor moved their eyes;
It had been strange, even in a dream,
To have seen those dead men rise.

It was a poem that had always fascinated Mary. The mariner killing an albatross with his crossbow and dooming the crew of his ship. The haunting of the mariner by the ghosts of his comrades. She did not know it now, but she would incorporate many of the themes of Coleridge's poem into the novel she would write. And now, in this realm of the departed, the melancholy she felt would be augmented by the sheer terror of the possible reanimation of the dead.

Natsumi was not likewise fascinated. Visions of the internment camps returned, coupled with descriptions she had read of the devastation at Nagasaki and Hiroshima. Walking through the valley of the shadow of death? Yes, she did fear the evil—the evil that men do to other men—and women, and children, and future generations. She remembered one tragic day at the Camp Forest prisoner of war camp when an elderly Asian man was shot and killed for trying to escape. The incident was never reported. There were murders at other camps that later became a matter of public record:

—Kanesaburo Oshima shot in the back of the head at Fort Still, Oklahoma.
—Toshio Kobata and Hiroto Isomura killed by shotgun blast at Lordsburg, New Mexico.
—James Ito and Katsuji Kanegawa shot during an uprising at the Manzanara concentration camp in California.
—James Hatsuaki Wakasa shot trying to leave Topaz center without a pass.
—Shoichi James Okamoto shot at Tule Lake segregation center for not showing his pass to a sentry.

Natsumi did not know their names but she knew their passing had been unfair and she knew the pain it had caused friends, family, even casual acquaintances. This corridor of bones brought it all back.

Ríona felt like the empire of death was closing in on her. The myriad array of skulls reminded her of the world she had left, depopulated in part by the horrific pandemic (brought there by Riordan and Mac Conmara, although she could not be sure of this). This memory and the recent observation of the destruction of the Twin Towers overwhelmed her. The flickering torchlight and the claustrophobic hallways of the catacombs pressed in on her like a heavy weight. She had trouble breathing and clung to Riordan as they followed the others through the tunnel.

For his part, Riordan shared some of Mary Wollstonecraft's fascination with the macabre arrangements of fleshless bodies. The soul lived in the bones. It was released upon death…usually but not always. He had never seen a soul but now the opportunity might arise. For him the flickering torchlight was hypnotic. There—was that a departed consciousness taking form and flying from this miserable place? Flying to a heavenly home…or escaping across the veil to roam the earth for eternity? These were not helpful thoughts. Ríona needed his support, not his foolish fantasies.

At each juncture where the tunnel split off in two directions, McGinley and Mac Conmara had a brief conference. There was no indication that an exit existed at the end of one or the other. They examined the dust on the tunnel floor for footprints or other marks of recent passage. They watched the smoke of the torch when held into one or the other corridor to see if a breeze might indicate fresh air. In the end they simply picked a direction based on intuition. Little better than flipping a coin. Lost in a labyrinth or more properly, a maze, they might wander here until thirst made them delirious. The torch would not last forever and once it was extinguished…

"Master," Riordan said to Mac Conmara the alchemist, "I hear something up ahead." They had just come to another intersection.

There was a sound like the creaking of old wheels that needed oiling in the corridor to their right. It was either salvation in the form of a human who, they hoped, knew the way out, or some supernatural demon that would end their suffering one way or another. Should they go to the left or to the right?

"Why don't you run up ahead and see who or what that is while we wait here?" Mac Conmara told his apprentice. It was not actually a question.

Riordan took the very last match and clutching it in a cupped hand, lit it and ventured forth. A few hundred yards along the tunnel which, to make matters worse, turned and twisted and changed levels abruptly, Riordan came to a barricade. This was just a series of wooden planks standing vertically to block the passage and Riordan could see through slits between the boards. On the other side, light from a torch illuminated a chamber. Inside, a man was unwrapping long shapes which, to Riordan's fantastic imagination, resembled human bodies. And of course, they were human bodies.

The match had burned down and touched Riordan's palm, burning the skin. He howled at the sudden pain. The man on the other side of the barrier heard this and rushed to the wall of planks. "Qui est là?" he demanded. Riordan got the idea and answered, "Is ainm dom Riordan," in Gaelic before he thought the better of responding to what might be a flesh-eating demon. The man gave out a low growl, confused by the words he did not understand. But this was enough to send Riordan scurrying back, albeit it bumping into walls and tripping every few feet.

Reaching the intersection where the others waited, Riordan blurted out his story between gasps for breath. The story concerned a monster, seven or eight feet tall, that was stripping the flesh from cadavers and popping bits of it into his mouth as he worked. No one actually believed him, save maybe Mary Wollstonecraft. A Monster! Delicious! As it turned out, the barricade was in fact a makeshift door and the monster of Riordan's imagination skillfully pulled this open and pursued the strange foreigner who had invaded the catacombs presumably without authorization. A jiggling torchlight came through the twists and turns of the corridor and soon the time travelers stood face to face with Riordan's monster.

"Oh," said Mary, "he's kind of cute."

"Qui es-tu et que fais-tu ici?" asked André Lemaire.

Mary translated for the others and then explained to André, without going into much detail, that they were travelers, English and American, and they had gotten lost in the catacombs. Which entrance had they used, André wanted to know. Mary raked her memory for the entrance she had heard about as a child when the sights of Paris had been narrated to her by cousins who had visited here. She muttered, "Um, by the cathedral." Since there were many cathedrals and just as many possible stairways beneath them leading to the tunnels, André shrugged and gave up his interrogation.

"You will want to be following me out when I exit. For the next half hour, please remain here as I have unfinished work to do before I can leave. I will come back for you," André told Mary.

After he had left the intersection and Mary had related André's request to the others, Riordan said, "See? I told you…he is eating those bodies!"

"Silly boy," said Mary. "He is not *my* idea of a monster. And after all, this is a sepulcher. You would expect to find bodies down here. Not just bones."

Sometime later, guided by André Lemaire, the time travelers emerged from the musty gloom of the ossuary. André had led them past the entrance at the Barrier l'Enfer in order to avoid meeting up with the Inspector and had taken them to a stairway at Le Cimetière du Sud in Montparnasse. This came up by an old windmill which sat at the center of the cemetery, built by the monks of the Brothers of Charity in the seventeenth century. Le Cimetière du Sud will one day be one of the largest cemeteries in Paris containing the graves of many famous people: Charles Baudelaire, Constantin Brancusi, Alfred Dreyfus, Camille Saint-Saëns, Guy de Maupassant, Man Ray, César Frank, Tristan Tzara, Susan Sontag, Charles Garnier, Chaïm Soutine, Gyula Brassaï, and Jean-Paul Sartre, to name a few. But not yet.

André bade them au revoir. He had enlightened them as to the date: July 15, 1815. It will be on this day that Napoleon Bonaparte will surrender and be transported on the HMS *Bellerphon* to England and subsequently become exiled to Saint Helena.

This is also the year Mary Wollstonecraft had visited Germany and was waylaid by the misty space-time anomaly. She has been missing from the Friedrichstraße castle in Germany since May. She now has the option of returning to Germany, or to England, although the thought of crossing the channel on a packet boat ship once again is irksome. Yet, opportunity calls.

"Oh Hell," said Mary, "which is the way to Calais?"

They had found, with some difficulty, a depot on the Boulevard du Montparnasse where the boarding of a diligence coach was to take place within the hour. The coach company ran a daily to Lyons and a special every third day to Calais. Luckily, this was the day for the coach to Calais. Everyone had decided to see Mary Wollstonecraft off on her return to England and so the group waited as preparations for the journey took place. As they waited, McGinley and Natsumi went into a boucherie around the corner to procure a box of edibles: cuisses de poulet that were fried and some sandwiches of jambon et fromage that were wrapped in paper by the boucher. When it came time to pay, Natsumi brought out a hand full of coins: twentieth century American money. The boucher selected a few silver coins and said, "Merci."

"Well, that went well," said Natsumi. "I wasn't sure they would take our money."

"Looks like we got all this for 75 cents," said McGinley. I feel like we cheated that man."

"How much is 75 cents worth in 1815? He probably got a good deal."

The diligence coach (Mary thought it inferior to the British stagecoach counterpart) was a large, sturdily built carriage pulled by four or sometimes six Norman horses which could seat six to eight people inside and which could carry many pounds of luggage atop its roof. The large pile of boxes and chests were secured by chains or ropes and covered with a canvas tarp. This gave the conveyances a top-heavy appearance, although they rarely toppled over. Added to this mass was additional roof seating where another half-dozen travelers could ride, albeit subject to the elements. The interior passenger section sat on leather thongs instead of springs which gave it a relatively smooth ride compared to the English stagecoach. It was decorated inside with green velvet trappings. The diligence coach, pulled by enough of the strong draft animals, could achieve speeds of six or seven miles per hour.

"Master," said Riordan to the alchemist as they waited and watched the coach being loaded and the horses hitched up, "I was thinking…what if we went along with the lady to England. We could be of service to her and, what is more, we could then travel to Ireland. It would not be the Ireland of our own era, but it would still be our native home."

"But Riordan," answered Mac Conmara, "the cost! How would we pay the fare for the packet boat, much less for the coach?"

"Mister Mac Conmara," said Mary, "I would be very happy to lend you the funds. I would very much enjoy your company. The channel crossing is dreadful enough when you are among friends, but alone…"

Natsumi and McGinley had just returned with the food. "Could we go along too," asked Natsumi. "At least to Calais…to see them off?"

"Perhaps if we all stay together," answered McGinley, "we would have a better chance of once again encountering a time vortex. You never know when one of those things will pop up."

It was decided. Natsumi, McGinley, and Mac Conmara, being older than the others, took seats inside the carriage while Mary, Ríona, and Riordan climbed to the top of the diligence to the seating area called the Imperial. The coachman sat just in front on the Imperial and cracked his long whip in the air above the horses. Besides the time travelers there were eight other passengers, a conductor, and two postilions, or post-boys, who rode on the left-side horses for better control of the team. The Norman horses were a cross between small horses called bidets and large Roman mares and were spirited and robust. They were each adorned with a set of silver bells which jingled an announcement as they entered a village on the road.

They crossed the Seine at Neuilly-sur-Seine and proceeded north through Saint-Denis. The horses were exchanged for a fresh team at Chambly, a small village in the department of Oise in the region of Hauts-de-France about 35 km north of Paris. When they had been driving for a total of nine hours at a pace that would have exhausted most draft animals, they reached the outskirts of Beauvais. Here they would stop for the night at a small inn which catered to diligence coach travelers.

The town of nearly 13,000 people, boasted of having the highest Gothic cathedral ever built, Cathédrale Saint-Pierre de Beauvais. Near the cathedral on old streets around the Place de l'Hôtel de Ville were houses dating from the 12th century and the remains of ancient ramparts. The town site at the confluence of the Thérain and Avelon Rivers, was bordered by rolling hills of chestnut and elm and fringed with fields of sunflowers. Tapestries produced in Beauvais for over 2,000 years displayed colors picked from the natural beauty of the area.

Now most of the department of Oise was occupied by British troops, fresh from their victory over Napoleon at Waterloo, and Beauvais saw its share of the red coated soldiers. Some of them were drinking and singing loudly at the inn when the travelers arrived. The inn, called l'Auberge de Jeanne Hachette, was named after a local heroine, Jeanne Laisné or Fourquet, who had the nickname of Jean the Hatchet because she had brandished an axe during a battle in 1472 with the invading troops of Charles the Bold, Duke of Burgundy, and had helped to prevent the British takeover of the town. The irony of this was apparently lost on the British soldiers.

Mary, Ríona, and Riordan joined two of their younger fellow travelers, a French couple of newlyweds named Roseline and Gustave Baudin, for a drink in the dining room of l'Auberge de Jeanne Hachette. A nosey celebration was underway.

"Here's to Wellington," yelled one British soldier over the clamor of the drunken celebration. "Here, here," returned another and this was echoed throughout the room.

Mary was delighted to see so many of her countrymen and yet, when she smiled at a handsome young soldier at an adjacent table, the man rose and strolled, unsteadily because somewhat inebriated, over to her table.

" 'Tis a British lass, me good fellows," he shouted back to his companions. "None of these Frenchy wenches that spit in our ale and give us who knows what diseases." And to Mary: "Hallo, me lady. Give us a kiss."

Mary responded with a well-aimed shove that sent the soldier sprawling upon the wooden floor. Laughter came from the soldier's table. A second soldier now approached. He accosted Ríona.

"Little lady, help us celebrate our illustrious victory," he said.

Gustave Baudin then rose from his chair and hurled a mug of ale at the man's face. "Pour qui tut te prends?" he yelled at the man. "Ca suffit!"

Riordan now rose. "There is an old Irish saying, my good fellow," he said. "It goes, 'Is minic a gheibhean beal oscailt diog duntal.' It means, an open mouth often catches a closed fist."

The soldiers at the next table were no longer laughing. In unison they stood and glared at Riordan and company. It seemed appropriate to forestall what might be an unpleasant encounter by retreating to their rooms, and so the time travelers did so.

The French, Baudin later told Mary, had had enough of war. They were tired and had been invaded by the British and the Prussians and the Dutch and now showed little resistance. Some supported the Emperor, some supported the King, and so loyalties confused every issue. These foreign troops would soon leave, and order would be restored to France. It was unlikely, he said, that there would ever be another revolution. The next day, Mary translated this for Riordan and Ríona as they sat on the rocking and swaying Imperial as the coach ventured up the road. Riordan, who had studied history during his stay in the twentieth century, knew better that revolution was only a few decades away, but he had the wisdom to keep quiet about the truth—the truth of his own version of reality.

A late lunch was had in the city of Amiens at la Maison de Manon Roland (named for Marie-Jeanne Roland de la Platière, a French Revolutionary figure of the Girondist party, a salonnière and writer, who lived in Amiens in the latter half of the eighteenth century). Mary ordered pâté de canard d'Amiens (duck pâté in pastry) followed by la ficelle Picarde (a cheese-topped crêpe with ham and mushroom filling). This may have seemed extravagant to the others who settled for fried goat cheese and fresh bread, but Mary explained that, although the French had many faults, cooking was not one of them.

There was time for a quick stroll to see the famous Notre-Dame Cathedral, one of the largest in France and considered archetypical of the often flamboyant Gothic style. Riordan was feeling a bit like a tourist, but he was impressed by the lofty façade with its triple arches and sculptures of the Saints and of Christ presiding over the day of the Last Judgement.

"And did you know," said Mary, as they examined the main entrance to the cathedral, "that this great monument was originally built as a resting place for what the Templars brought back from the Fourth Crusade? Jacques de Moray would not admit to it, but here was stored a reliquary containing the head of John the Baptist! Somehow, it disappeared, but it was there in the thirteenth century."

"You are so knowledgeable, Mary," commented Natsumi, not hiding her sarcasm. "How do you know so much about this place?"

"I read," Mary replied. "I submerge myself in literature and in histories. Did you also know that this town, Amiens, was the home of Pierre Ambroise François Choderlos de Laclos? He was a novelist, and an army general, and wrote one of my favorite books, *Les Liaisons Dangereuses*."

The diligence coach was waiting not far from the cathedral in the Saint-Leu quarter. Again sitting atop the coach, Mary, Ríona, and Riordan had a view of old red brick buildings that dated to medieval times and of the Canal de la Somme, a waterway encompassing the Somme River and man-made extensions, which ran all the way to the English Channel at Saint-Valery-sur-Somme. Their route followed the canal through the countryside of the Picardy region, taking them to Abbeville, the last stop on their journey to Calais.

On the Paris Road into Abbeville they passed Château d'Eaucourt-sur-Somme, the ruins of a castle that was erected around the start of the 15th century, and Château de Bagatelle, built in the middle of the 1700s by a textile industrialist. Gustave Baudin told them that in 1346, Edward III's army crossed the Somme River at Abbeville on its way to the Battle of Crécy. Napoleon stayed in the town on 18 June 1803 and visited the camp of Boulogne where he planned an expedition to England. In 1814 when an invasion was expected from the British, the Germans and the Dutch, the urban National Guard was reorganized all across the Empire. 30 pieces of artillery were installed on the walls at Abbeyville.

It was a place that currently had seen many comings and goings. During the First Restoration, 10,000 British troops passed through Abbeville to return to their country. Louis XVIII entered the town in April 1814 to cheers and adulations. In March 1815, King Louis XVIII then on his way to exile in Ghent, spent a night in the town. When the King returned to France after Napoleon's defeat to ensure his second restoration, he arrived at Cambrai very near Abbeville. All those auspicious arrivals and departures of the famous and powerful testified to Abbeville's strategic location in that region of Picardy.

Another town, another cathedral, another inn, another restaurant, more British troops as the journey neared its end. Tonight's fare included a shared flamiche, a pie filled with chopped leeks, crème fraîche, and a bit of goat cheese, followed by Carré d'Agneau de Pré Salé rôti aux fines herbes, a rack of the region's unique salt marsh lamb cooked with vegetables and les fines herbs (parsley, tarragon, chives, and chervil), and ending with cheeses: a soft Abbaye de Belval, a spicy baguette Laonnaise, and a strongly aromatic Maroilles.

"Well, one thing is certain," said Mary, "there are some things I'll miss about France."

"What," said Natsumi, "not anxious to get home to mutton stew?"

The next day riding in the coach McGinley chided Natsumi for her treatment of Mary Wollstonecraft.

"She may be a famous author," replied Natsumi, "but she sure is a bitch!"

They drove through the fishing village of Boulogue-sur-Mer and the tiny hamlet of Coquelles. The road was filled with British soldiers marching less sharply than they should, some weary, some wounded, some worried about returning home to an unfaithful wife or a distressed business. A malaise possessed them, a despondence spawned of the futility of war, the guilt of survival, the sudden loss of the engagement and conflict that had nourished them, the shock of quietude. It showed in their lethargic progress, their stooped attitudes, their muddled gate. No one cheered them as they passed.

The coach entered the outskirts of Calais. Located on the Pas de Calais, the boundary between the English Channel and North Sea, Calais was a major port for trading, smuggling, and the transport of troops between England and France. She was part of the Côte d'Opale or Opal Coast, and shared the same high, white cliffs as the English coast at Dover, only 25 miles across the channel. Calais was a territory of England from 1347 to 1558. Under British rule, many of the old streets had names like Hemp Street, Cutle Street, Corket Street, Pickering Street, and White Hall Lane. The reconquest of Calais by Francis, Duke of Guise, took place in 1558, and now she was French.

Still, the connection to England remained strong. When Anne Boleyn was executed within the Tower of London on 19 May of 1536, she had requested that the headsman of Calais end her life. He used a sword contrary to British beheading tradition. Just this January of 1815, the once elegant Lady Emma Hamilton was buried in the timber yard at Calais. In 1801, when living scandalously with the married but separated Admiral Horatio Lord Nelson, she had given birth to his daughter. Nelson was killed by a French snipper during the Battle of Trafalgar in 1805 and although he had made a will providing for Lady Hamilton's care, she received nothing and died in poverty.

Calais: the Église Notre-Dame Cathedral (in the English style), the Tour du Guet Watch Tower situated on Calais Nord at the Places d'Armes and dating from 1229, Hôtel Meurice de Calais which catered to English elite, the Hôtel d'Angleterre ready for wealthy travelers from Paris, the brasseries, the bistros, the boulangeries, the quays, the busy waterfront. The time travelers, however, had no time for sightseeing. A packet boat was about to depart.

Calais Nord was the oldest section of the town. It was effectively an island, being surrounded by canals that connected it with the English Channel. There, overlooked by the Tour du Guet, were the town's wharfs. At the Bassin Carot was the Dock Fournier. Thick braided ropes ran from the moorings to the packet *Roxanne.* A gangplank had been extended between the dock and the *Roxanne's* deck. She was a small sailing ship carrying mail, cargo, and less than a dozen passengers. The diligence coach pulled up next to the gangplank.

"Oh, Hell," said Mary Wollstonecraft, "I hope there is a decent salon. Somewhere to hide from the elements…and the other passengers."

"Lorcan Mac Conmara turned to Madison McGinley. 'I guess this is goodbye." He said. McGinley looked at Natsumi. Natsumi gave him a small nod and a big smile.

"I think, seeing as we have come all this way together, we had better not separate. England will suit us just fine."

"You are all to come and stay with me at Bishopsgate," said Mary. "At least until Percy and Claire and I take our trip back to Lake Geneva in Switzerland." Natsumi rolled her eyes—hasn't she had enough of the continent by now, she wondered?

Most civilian travel between England and France had been suspended during the war and only now, with the return of the King, had it resumed. Most channel shipping was still for troop carrying or for smuggling. But, with passenger services potentially a major source of income for the coastal shipping industry, the packet boats were back and being outfitted with pleasurable amenities. Yes, the *Roxanne* had a salon and the salon had a fully stocked bar. The time travelers mounted the gangplank and boarded the *Roxanne.* Mary headed for the salon.

The *Roxanne* was a fore-and-aft rigged gaff ketch with two mainsails and mizzenmasts. The crew set the sails and cast off from the pier, catching the wind just right to come about and sail up the Avanti Canal to the English Channel. Once she entered the channel things changed dramatically. The prevailing winds tried to push the ship back into the harbor. The *Roxanne* therefore tacked against the wind which put her into the troughs of the channel's waves. She rolled. She rocked. She picked up speed and came about, tacking in the opposite direction. This would be the pattern for the eighteen-hour trip. The effect on the passengers was not pleasurable.

Dr. Madison McGinley had an excellent view of the briny deep as he leaned over the rail. He was in the position to watch the white-tipped peaks splash against the hull, but he did not appreciate the swirling gray-green liquidity below him. He had company, however. Several other passengers had opted for fresh air. They clung to the rail like a murder of crows on a fence, and croaked in unison, dispensing their bodily fluids without regard for the direction of the wind. Some of the crew working the halyards chuckled at the sight of the seasick landlubbers.

Natsumi came on deck and put an arm around McGinley. She wanted to comfort him but this was probably a lost cause. "The others are down in the salon," she said. "The rolling isn't quite so bad down there. When you are feeling up to it…"

"I just need the fresh air, Natsumi. Thanks, but I'll be okay in a little bit."

They stood for a while, looking out over the channel, perhaps watching for an albatross, or at least, a sea gull. Nothing was in the air but the spray from the sea and a bank of gray clouds that seemed to have rolled off from the White Cliffs of Dover (you could see these on a clear day—only this wasn't a clear day). The clouds began to descend and almost touch the water. As McGinley and Natsumi watched, the air thickened and became a solid bank of mist. A familiar sort of mist.

"Do you think?" said Natsumi.

"Take my hand," said McGinley. "You never know where we may end up. I want to stay together."

In the salon no one was aware that the ship was sailing through mist that might or might not be a time rift. Casual conversation was taking place among the English-speaking passengers. Mac Conmara, Ríona, and Riordan sat off to one side of the salon on long wooden benches. Riordan tried to reassure Ríona:

"You will like Ireland," he said, "even in this century. It will remind you of your own home. We have wonderful hills of green where sheep graze, and wonderful cliffs overlooking the sea."

"Oh, Riordan," she answered, "I am so homesick."

"If only we hadn't lost the time machine," he said.

Mac Conmara nodded. "You could take Ríona home…assuming I could get the thing working correctly. That wasn't always the case."

"And you know what else I would like to do?" said Riordan. "I would like to go ahead in time to…I don't know exactly when…but, you remember that city where we saw the airplanes crash into the buildings? Well, if we could go to that time and place, maybe we could warn the people, or even stop the attack."

"Riordan, haven't you learned by now that you must never try to change time? That was horrible, that is true, but changing it might cause other things…"

"Nothing could be worse than that was." Riordan was certain changing that piece of history would be faultless. He said, "I'm going up on deck now to check on the Professor. I'll be right back."

Riordan climbed the short stairway from the salon to the deck and poked his head out just in time to see the mist rushing across the deck toward the group of seasick passengers at the rail. They were there…and then they were not there. As suddenly as it had come, the mist left. Riordan felt a moment of shock, disbelief, and then, as this kind of thing was not that unusual for the time travelers, he simply shook his head. Well, there they go, he thought. Goodbye and good luck.

Riordan was not sure whether he was glad that the mist had not taken him too, or whether he wished the entire ship had been whisked away to some other space-time. He was stuck now in 1815, but he would be going to Ireland with the love of his life. That was a good thing. He would miss the Professor and the woman. He hoped they would find themselves in a wonderful place, perhaps their own home. But he knew how indeterminate the time rift could be. How fickle. He sighed and returned to the salon.

Epilogue

The former Emperor, Napoleon Bonaparte, was still being held on the HMS *Bellerophon,* in route from Rochefort to Brixham. No one knew yet what to do with him. His accommodations in the great cabin were luxurious considering that he was a prisoner of war. He was allowed full range of the ship and often took long strolls along the deck. The *Bellerophon*, known as the "Billy Ruffen" by its crew, was a veteran of the French Revolution and the Napoleonic Wars, had fought in the Battle of Trafalgar, and was tasked with bringing home the body of Admiral Horatio Nelson. She had chased Napoleon all around the Atlantic for years and now, appropriately, she was his prison.

When Napoleon had surrendered to Captain Frederick Lewis Maitland on the *Bellerophon*, he had been treated with dignity and respect. The company of marines on the battleship stood at attention and the Captain bowed. Tonight there had been a sumptuous dinner in the great cabin. Rear-admiral Sir Henry Hotham had boarded the *Bellerophon* for the occasion. Afterward, Napoleon went on deck for his early evening stroll. Members of the crew who saw him took off their hats.

The former Emperor was short, 5 feet 6 inches, and had taken on considerable weight in recent years. He still wore the blue uniform, the gray cloak, and white breeches tucked into high black boots. On his head was perched the bicorne hat with a blue, white, and red cockade pinned to it. He walked with a swagger that bordered on a waddle and he might have looked from a distance like a large penguin negotiating a slippery ice float. He climbed to the poop deck where he watched as the French landscape slowly receded into the distance.

He started to return to his cabin when a strange sight met his battle-weary eyes. There, on the main deck, just beyond the mizzen mast, was an apparition—in fact, two apparitions. The ghosts of a man and a woman, translucent and wavering, appeared against the dim light of dusk. Who were these ghosts come to haunt him? What did they want? Their clothing was unusual. The woman was an Oriental. Napoleon, never one to shrink from conflict, decided to approach the ghosts and demand to know their intentions. As he neared them, the apparitions became momentarily solid, then faded in an instant and were gone. Too much Welsh rarebit, thought the Emperor. Too much wine. He shrugged and left the deck to retire early.

Thy cliffs, dear Dover! Harbour and hotel;
Thy custom-house, with all its delicate duties;
Thy waiters running mucks at every bell;
Thy packets, all whose passengers are booties
To those who upon land or water dwell;
And last, not least, to strangers uninstructed,
Thy long, long bills, whence nothing is deducted.
—"Don Juan," George Gordon Lord Byron, 1821

The packet *Roxanne* arrived at Dover early in the evening. Mary Wollstonecraft insisted Ríona, Riordan, and Mac Conmara join her for drinks at the Golden Anchor and afterward they would take rooms for the night at Wright's Hotel and Ship Inn across from the Granville Dock on Custom House Quay. "The stage to London," said Mary, "leaves at 6 in the morning, so be well rested."

Dover Road was 70 miles long and terminated at London Bridge on the Surrey side of the Thames River. Two locations along the road are worthy of mention (described in more detail in *A Tale of Two Cities* by Charles Dickens): Shooter's Hill and Blackheath. The former being dangerous as many a mail coach had been robbed there, and the latter being a favorite spot for assignations by heads of state and commoners alike. Shooter's Hill was known for a mineral spring where Queen Anne was said to have taken the waters during the eighteenth century, but it was much to be feared after sunset.

From London they traveled down the Old North Road to Surrey where in Englefield Green was to be found the neighborhood of Bishopsgate. Here Mary and Percy Shelley had rented a small cottage to which they would retire during the following year when they were not traveling. It was a two-story red brick house with a slate roof near Windsor Great Park, the private hunting grounds of Windsor Castle. Here Mary entertained Ríona, Riordan, and Mac Conmara. There were frequent visits from Percy Shelley and Claire Clairemont. It was all that Riordan could do to refrain from blurting out details of Mary's future to her. But Ireland beckoned and soon the time travelers parted ways.

The Express, an overland mail coach, left from The Swan with Two Necks at Lad Lane in London for Liverpool at 6 in the evening. It was a journey of over 24 hours. There were stops for fresh horses at Northampton, Leicester, and Stoke-on-Trent. The City of Dublin Packet Company ran a schooner (aptly called the *City of Dublin*) from Liverpool to the port on South Wall at Dublin. After 23 hours crossing the Irish Sea, the travelers disembarked at the Pigeon House where they were confronted by customs officials. There was some concern about their lack of luggage, but they were released when it became clear that they were Irish citizens. After this, the trip into the city was by a coach called the Ringsend Car, in which 16 passengers were jostled uncomfortably for a ride that took them up Great Brunswick Street, past Trinity College, and into the Temple Bar district.

Usher's Quay ran along the Liffey River a few blocks west of where the coach had left them off. Fronted on the river was a large building with a rambling portico of Doric columns. An expansive area inside served as the public Wellesley Market, and adjacent to this was Home's Hotel, a 200 room establishment that boasted, "The charges are low and no gratuity is allowed to be given to the servants for their attendance." Perfect, as the travelers were getting low on the funds advanced to them by Mary Wollstonecraft.

There was a coffee house in the lobby of the hotel. The travelers convened there to recuperate from their arduous road trip and to discuss their plans.

"What do you think of Dublin?" Riordan asked Ríona.

"Well, at least there are no tall buildings into which airplanes might crash and explode," she said.

"I don't think we have enough money left to get us to Cork," said Mac Conmara. "We'll have to think about how to raise some funds."

"Why go to Cork?" asked Riordan. "I like Dublin myself. It's a nice big city with lots of pubs and a big college and the people all seem nice. I remember when I grew up in Innishannon in the County Cork by the River Bandon, how the people there were not always very nice. And at

Cork it was all about the Church…the bloody Catholic Church…murdering Protestants in Paris and so forth, and about the Clans in Kerry and…"

"I wonder myself," said Mac Conmara, "if my old castle is still up in the hills. My workshop…"

"And the dog, Teige. He would be about 125 years old by now, so I guess that's a stupid thing to say. You know," Riordan continued, "if we stay in this time frame, in another 25 years there will be a horrible famine. The potato crop is going to get the blight and the British aren't going to help us get through it. Many of our people will immigrate to America."

"I keep forgetting you are a history buff. At least we would know and be able to prepare for that. Any other insights into the history that awaits us?"

"I don't know if I like the big city," said Ríona. "I'd like to see those green hills and the sheep that you talked about."

"Then it is to Cork we will go," said Mac Conmara. "Let us look for work first thing in the morning. There is a waterfront here and a shipping industry. Surely we can get something."

"Oh rats!" said Riordan.

As they left the coffee house and returned to the lobby of the hotel, Riordan suddenly stopped and stared at a bronze plaque that was affixed to the wall. "Say. Master." He said to Mac Conmara, "isn't this 1815?"

"It certainly was when we were at Mary's cottage in Bishopsgate. Why?"

"Look at this plaque."

He did. It read: "Home's Hotel, proprietor George C. Homes, established 1823."

"And look at that newspaper on the stand over there. The date…"

The date on the front page of the Dublin Evening Post was June 18, 1831. The headline read: "Police take possession of Roman Catholic priest's cattle—Thirteen dead, twenty wounded." The article went on to say that the enforcement of tithes on the Roman Catholic majority to support the Anglican Church of Ireland was now resulting in violence. It had begun with a priest in Kilkenny convincing his parishioners to place their cattle in his care to avoid the compulsory tithe to the English church. That had been in May. Now resisters in Wexford County had been fired upon by yeomen.

"Master," said Riordan, "how can it be 1831? I haven't seen any mist or anything unusual, at least not since the channel crossing. But at Bishopsgate the papers there said it was 1815."

"I don't know, Riordan. Maybe during the voyage across the Irish Sea when we slept something happened. The date changed but the place did not. That is certainly different. Keep an open eye. Time may be accelerating without our being aware of it."

"The schism between Ireland and England is certainly accelerating. And the potato famine is just around the corner!"

The ghosts appeared again, only this time not on a ship, and they were not really ghosts. The misty space-time vortex, a whirlwind of time rifts, had toyed with Natsumi and McGinley, materializing them in this era or that, then snatching them away practically before they could blink. The interval of momentary stasis was increasing so that they now had a longer glimpse of their location before the whirlwind took them again.

"Watch for something that looks like the twentieth century," said McGinley. "If we see it, we jump!"

Someplace with a lot of sand and a long line of sweating people pulling large stone blocks with ropes materialized briefly. Then this scene was replaced by that of a square in which rose St. Peter's Basilica. King Henry V was kissing the feet of Pope Paschal II; the year was 1111. The King wished to be crowned emperor, but the Pope refused. Henry would capture and imprison the holy Father and force him to do so. Turmoil. The whirlwind loved turmoil.

Next there appeared a partially finished five-sided fort of brick sitting on top of a sand bar reinforced with granite. It had walls five feet thick and gun emplacements three tiers high. Impressive, but the fort was under siege. The date was April 12, 1861. The fort, named after Revolutionary War hero General Thomas Sumter, was the Union stronghold, Fort Sumter. Confederate forces were about to fire on it for the next 34 hours. It was the beginning of the American Civil War.

More whirling of temporal winds. Now they looked out on the town of Villach in northern Italy. A rockslide was burying the town in rubble, destroying other villages nearby. It was the aftershock of a 6.9-magnitude earthquake felt as far away as Pisa and Naples and Rome where there was damage to the Basilica of Santa Maria Maggiore. The Friuli earthquake was taking place in 1348, contemporary with the beginning of the Black Death in Europe. In the minds of many, this was the beginning of the Biblical Apocalypse.

Whirl, whirl, whirl. Long Beach Municipal Auditorium in Long Beach, California, June 28, 1952. Screen actress Piper Laurie was placing the crown of Catherine the Great of Russia (on loan to the pageant) on the head of Armi Helena Kuusela of Finland at the very first Miss Universe Pageant. Miss Kuusela was the daughter of a Finnish sausage merchant. She was 17 years of age, weighed 110 pounds, and her measurements were 34-23-34. She would earn a seven-year motion picture contract. The first, second, third, and fourth runner ups were, respectively, Miss Hawaii, Miss Greece, Miss Hong Kong, and Miss Germany. One-piece swimsuits, banners with the names of their countries, bright eyes, and white teeth—as the young ladies gathered for a picture op, Natsumi and McGinley jumped from the whirlwind.

The Seneca and the Cayuga tell that the Great Spirit looked down with favor at the homeland of the Iroquois and offered his blessing by placing his fingers upon the sacred ground. The ten long impressions filled with water and clear lakes came into being. The white man came later and called these the Finger Lakes (actually there are eleven in all). The Onondaga and Oneida tribes lived in the region as well. Also the Mohawk. At the tip of the lake named after the Seneca was the town of Seneca Falls where the women's suffrage movement was born. South of the lake near the border between New York and Pennsylvania was the city of Elmira.

At Elmira was a Union army camp, Camp Rathbun, converted into a Civil War prisoner of war camp in the summer of 1864. Over 12,000 Confederate soldiers were incarcerated there. Nearly 3,000 died of disease, malnutrition, or exposure to the severe winter weather. In the 1870s and 80s, Mark Twain spent summers vacationing at Quarry Farm in Elmira. He wrote *The Adventures of Tom Sawyer, The Prince and the Pauper, Life on the Mississippi, Adventures of Huckleberry Finn, and A Connecticut Yankee in King Arthur's Court* during that time.

On a Sunday in November of 1963, in a small farmhouse off Jerusalem Hill Road just east of Elmira proper, Wayland Delany sat in his Laz-Z-Boy recliner watching his new Zenith Console color television. It was just too cold to go outside although the driveway needed shoveling. Wayland had come to the Finger Lakes region over ten years ago after a series of adventures in time travel. These are documented in the book, *The Death of Time.* Now that he had had a decade of R and R, he was getting a bit restless.

Wayland had been thirteen when his mother, Francis Delaney, moved to Oak Ridge, Tennessee in 1943 to devote herself to the war effort. Francis Delaney had been one of the women that had worked on the Manhattan Project at Oak Ridge. In 1952, with an interest in science and a good aptitude for learning, Wayland applied to the newly opened Oak Ridge School of Reactor Technology at Oak Ridge National Laboratory. As part of his studies in Reactor Hazards Analysis Wayland was apprenticed to Dr. Madison James McGinley at the lab. McGinley had developed a device for traveling through time. The rest was history.

Wayland's wife, Betty Anne, was making snickerdoodles in the kitchen. The sweet aroma of the cookies as they baked in the hot oven reached Wayland. Soon there would be warm cookies to munch. He worked the lever on the Laz-Z-Boy that brought up the leg support and leaned back. He pointed the remote at the Zenith and switched the channel to CBS. A special report was being broadcast.

It was the 24th of November. Two days ago, the news had reported the assassination of President John F. Kennedy during a motorcade through Dealey Plaza in Dallas, Texas. Police had arrested Lee Harvey Oswald for the shooting and were holding him for arraignment. This morning, Oswald was to be transferred from police headquarters to the county jail. Television crews were present and live coverage showed the accused murderer being led through a corridor. Jack Ruby, a local nightclub owner, suddenly sprang into the scene and fired a handgun at Oswald. There was pandemonium.

When Betty Anne entered the living room with a plate of the freshly baked cookies, she found Wayland beside himself with emotion. "If only…" he mumbled. "If only what?" she asked. "Never mind," he replied. Now she looked at the TV, listened to the news report, and she understood.

"Somethings just are what they are," she said. "There is nothing you can do about them. These are just strange times."

"I guess you're right,' said Wayland. He got some ice from the freezer, working the metal lever to pop the cubes up from the ice tray, deposited a handful in a tall glass, twisted the top from a bottle of coke and poured this into the glass. Too early in the day to add a little rum. Although a Cuba libra seemed appropriate somehow, given the conspiracy theories involving Castro's roll in Kennedy's death that were surfacing.

The next day, Wayland went to the tool shed to get the snowblower out. Damn lot of snow this year, he thought. Good old Briggs and Stratton engine on this baby never fails to start no matter how cold it is. Just prime it a bit and pull the starter cord and...broom, broom, brooom! Watch that snow fly. Only today, the B & S didn't cooperate. What kind of BS is this? Check the gas. Yep, okay. Ignition on? Of course. Oh shit! Should have bought the one with the electric starter. He rolled the damn thing back into the shed and got out a snow shovel.

Just as Wayland turned to start shoveling, a groaning noise like a dying bull met his ears. There was the smell of ozone in the air and a slight shimmer to what he could see through the snow that had begun to fall. There was something up ahead on the drive, something big and black and round and...somehow familiar. He dropped the shovel and ran to the object, put his hands on it. Warm even through his heavy gloves. It was, it must be, the time machine.

The last time, and the only time that Wayland had seen the time machine had been on a distant planet in a distant future when he had helped McGinley and company try to stop the scientist, Nikolai Borisov, from traveling back in time to the origins of the universe, the Big Bang as it was called. He and the alchemist, Lorcan Mac Conmara and the alchemist's apprentice, Riordan Ó Ciardha had entered the evil scientist's laboratory using a time bubble and materialized just as Borisov was getting ready to activate the time machine. Mac Conmara and Riordan had ended up inside the machine with Borisov as it made its leap into the past, and Wayland had been coldcocked by the scientist's guards back in the laboratory.

As far as Wayland knew, nobody knew what the fate of those in the time machine had been. It was obvious that the universe had not ended, so it was reasonable to assume that Mac Conmara and Riordan had been successful in stopping the scientist. Did that mean that they were inside this thing? Had they come to fetch him, to take him on new adventures? Did they have something specific in mind, for instance, returning to the day Kennedy was shot and stopping Oswald? Wouldn't that be something!

Wayland found the handle that opened the door from the outside. He hesitated for a minute—just a minute. Then he slid the door open and looked inside. Empty! His mind began to race through the possibilities. Were they dead? Had they sent the time machine to him somehow? Was this purely an accident of fate? He looked at the control panel. Could he figure it out? Could he take the machine back in time and save Kennedy? Wayland entered the time machine.

Afterword

One hopes that the alchemist, his apprentice, and the apprentice's girlfriend made it back to their own time and that Scheherazade the cat was there to greet them. Or that the acceleration of time returned to normal and the trio found a new life in the ever-wondrous city of Dublin. One never knows what Mother Time has in store. No doubt McGinley and Natsumi returned to Oak Ridge. And Wayland Delaney? The chances are he won't figure out how to pilot the time machine. Probably.

I have taken a few liberties with the activities of Mary Shelley in this story. I have her touring Europe alone with her cousin, Claire Clairmont, but in fact, Mary and Claire were accompanied by Percy Bysshe Shelley on the trip. Mary and Percy published *History of a Six Weeks' Tour* in 1817 which I referenced for her descriptions of the river journey in my story. Upon their return to England, Mary was pregnant. Percy Shelley's wife, Harriet committed suicide in 1816, and then he and Mary married. The couple had four children together, only one of whom survived. It is possible that Percy Shelley was also the father of Claire Clairmont's child although Claire had a shaky affair with Lord Byron at the famous outing in Switzerland when Mary began writing *Frankenstein.* Percy died in a sailing accident in 1822. Besides *Frankenstein or The Modern Prometheus*, Mary Shelley went on to publish several more works including *Valperga*, *Perkin Warbeck*, *The Last Man*, *Lodore*, and *Falkner.* She died in 1851.

You can tour the Paris Catacombs, some of it. For a history of the Paris underground and to get an idea of the extent of the tunnels, visit www.explographics.com. There are many historical maps and interesting anecdotes on the site. For a large, detailed, annotated map of the underground which shows the old mines and the various catacomb rooms (also produced by Explographics) go to https://www.reddit.com/r/Maps/comments/2ejjr1/parisian_catacombs_7000_x_7000/. Philibert Aspairt was a real person who was lost in the catacombs during 1793 and not found until 11 years later. His tomb is located in the catacombs on the spot where his body was found.

The Holy Grail has been a subject for speculative literature since at least the 12th century. In *Perceval, le Conte du Graal* (*The Story of the Grail*) by Chrétien de Troyes, it is represented as a deep dish or bowl containing a single communion wafer which was presented by a beautiful maiden at a dinner hosted by the legendary Fisher King. In *Parzival* by Wolfram von Eschenbach, the grail was kept at a castle, which now is sometimes identified as a Benedictine monastery in Montserrat in Catalonia. It is no longer there if ever it was. Robert de Boron tells us in *Joseph d'Arimathie* that Joseph of Arimathea obtained the chalice of the Last Supper and used it to collect Christ's blood as He was removed from the cross. To protect the sacred object, Arimathea created a society of Grail keepers, which later included Knight Perceval of King Arthur's court.

There are several Grail related relics that have been identified as such by believers. The *Sacro Catino,* Sacred Basin, or Genoa Chalice, a green glass dish at the Genoa Cathedral, is said to have been used at the Last Supper. The Holy Chalice of Valencia is an agate dish with a mounting for such use as a chalice. The Nanteos Cup, a medieval wooden bowl also thought to be the Grail was found near Rhydyfelin, Wales. And so forth. It makes one think, doesn't it, of the scene in the movie, *Indiana Jones and the Last Crusade*, where Jones must select the real Grail from an assortment guarded by a Templar Knight. The idea that Templars guarded the Grail probably originated in the 19th century in the writings of Joseph von Hammer-Purgstall.

On Friday the 13th of October 1307, King Philip IV of France ordered the arrest of Grand Master Jacques de Molay and several of his Templar Knights. They were imprisoned and tortured to make them confess to the trumped-up charges of idolatry, blasphemy, homosexual practices, and financial crimes. Morey and Geoffroi de Charney later retracted their confessions. They were burned at the stake in Paris in front of Notre Dame Cathedral on March 18, 1314. Morey cursed the King and the Pope saying, "Dieu sait qui a tort et a péché. Il va bientot arriver malheur à ceux qui nous ont condamnés à mort" ("God knows who is wrong and has sinned. Soon a calamity will occur to those who have condemned us to death"). Pope Clement died within the month and King Philip died in a hunting accident later that year.

Wei Shan may have been the Old General that Wang Wêi wrote about in his poem, "A Song of an Old General" although the poet apparently alluded therein to several generals of the Han Dynasty. Wei Shan was present at the Battle of Mobei in 119 BCE when Han forces attacked and bested the hordes of the Xiongnu. The Supreme Commanders for the Han were Wei Qing and Huo Qubing, favorites of Emperor Wu. In Japan, during the Yayoi Period (300 BCE to 250 CE), the island did conduct trading with China. It is entirely possible that our character, Iyo, could have traveled from Japan to the town of Jimo in the Shandong province. She might have ended up in the harem quarters at the Weiyang Palace in Chang'an. She is not a historical character, but her namesake was a successor to Queen Himiko, the Shaman empress of the Yamato Clan of the mid-200s CE.

Louis-Étienne Héricart de Thury was a real person who was director of the Paris Mine Inspection Service beginning in 1810. It was he who used old cemetery decorations and the stacking of skulls and femurs into patterns to enhance the ambiance of the catacombs. Amédée-Ernest Bollée (1844 –1917) was a Frenchman who built several steam-driven carriages including *La Mancelle, La Marie-Anne, La Nouvelle, La Rapide,* and *L'Obeissante* of our story. Home's Hotel in Dublin was opened by George Home in 1826. In 1840 it became a weaving factory and in 1848, an auction house. It was demolished around 1977. The Shelley's cottage in Bishopsgate in the Borough of Runnymede, Surrey, still stands.

About the Author

Byron Grush was born and raised in Naperville, Illinois, just southwest of Chicago. He is a third generation native of that town. Grush studied art and design at the University of Illinois and filmmaking at the School of the Art Institute of Chicago. At the Art Institute he was a student of Gregory Markopoulos, one of the originators of the New America Cinema movement in the 1960s.

Grush then taught at The School of the Art Institute of Chicago, creating a course in film animation in the mid-seventies. He later became an Associate Professor at the College of Art at Northern Illinois University in Dekalb, Illinois, where he taught in the Electronic Media area. He is the author of a book on hand-drawn animation techniques entitled *The Shoestring Animator*. Becoming interested in genealogy, he wrote a trilogy of historical novels based upon what he had learned about his early ancestors.

He and his wife moved to New Mexico in the late 1990s, and opened an art gallery called Muse Image which featured Outsider and Visionary Art in Santa Fe. They returned to the Midwest to retire in the small town of Delavan, Wisconsin, a place that reminds them of their roots. Grush's films are in the collection of the Chicago Film Archives. Grush writes, paints and studies Tai Chi.

Other fiction by Byron Grush

All The Way By Water
Once Upon a Gold Rush
Road of Stars
Dance Beneath A Diamond Sky
Violet at The Breakers: a novella
The New Unwritten Law: a novella
The Scrapple Eater: a novella
1954 or Just press the I Believe Button
Luncheon at the Dead Rat
The Death of Time

Short Story Collections by Byron Grush

Romeo's Revenge and Other Wisconsin Stories
The Cabinet of Curiosities of Barnaby Cannon and Other Stories

Nonfiction by Byron Grush

The Shoestring Animator

www.ingramcontent.com/pod-product-compliance
Lightning Source LLC
Chambersburg PA
CBHW071307130626
46556CB00004B/1505

* 9 7 8 0 9 9 8 5 4 5 4 5 5 *